Miss Bianca in the Antarctic

Miss Bianca in the Antarctic

Miss Bianca, possibly the most daring and accomplished heroine in mouse history, in this latest adventure falls into the greatest peril of even her career. While on an errand of mercy to the Antarctic with her loyal companion Bernard, she is stranded midst desolate wastes untrodden by the foot of man, with not a hope of rescue. Even Miss Bianca is daunted by this, but she soon embarks on a whirl of activity, converting the collected works of Shakespeare into a shelter against the icy blast, attending a ball with a group of friendly penguins, and pitting her wits against those of the tyrannical Emperor Penguin. You will not be surprised to hear, though, that the ever resourceful Miss Bianca at last finds her way home again – by a most unexpected means.

'This story holds a magic all its own.' *Western Mail*

MARGERY SHARP

Miss Bianca in the Antarctic

Illustrated by Erik Blegvad

Featuring characters from the Disney film suggested by the
books by Margery Sharp, *The Rescuers* and *Miss Bianca*
published by William Collins Sons & Co Ltd.

FONTANA · LIONS

First published in Great Britain in 1970 by William Heinemann Ltd
First published in Fontana Lions 1978
by William Collins Sons & Co Ltd
14 St James's Place, London SW1

© Margery Sharp
© Illustrations Erik Blegvad 1970

Made and printed in Great Britain by
William Collins Sons & Co Ltd Glasgow

Contents

CHAPTER I

No More Adventures

In the elegant pleasure-ground surrounding her
Porcelain Pagoda Miss Bianca, ex-Madam President
of the Mouse Prisoners' Aid Society, and her old
friend Bernard, its ex-Secretary, sat by the fountain
talking over old times. How many perilous adventures lay behind them! And not only along the
traditional MPAS lines of cheering prisoners in their
cells : Bernard and Miss Bianca had actually *rescued*
prisoners – to mention but three, a Norwegian poet
from the Black Castle, a girl-child from the Diamond
Palace, a boy-child from the Salt Mines! But now
Bernard was stout and grizzled, and Miss Bianca,
though her ermine coat still shone like silver, and
her huge brown eyes like topazes, lacked a little of
the agility necessary for dodging, for instance, blood-
hounds.

' 'Tis time for retirement indeed!' sighed she.

'I should jolly well think so,' said Bernard. 'I tell
you frankly, Miss Bianca, when I think of some of
the perils I've seen you in, my tail fairly freezes!'

'Who was ever at my side?' smiled Miss Bianca.
(Of course Bernard knew she meant him. Far from
freezing, his tail glowed down to the very tip.) 'And
yet what good, loyal friends and helpers we found,'
recalled Miss Bianca, 'even amongst bats!'

'I wonder what's become of old Nils?' mused

Bernard, referring to the Norwegian sailor-mouse who'd accompanied them to the Black Castle. Bernard and he had always got on together, they'd been practically best friends, but owing to the latter's seafaring way of life the connection hadn't been kept up.

'Good Nils!' murmured Miss Bianca. 'But come,' she added, flicking a drop of fountain-spray from her coat and adjusting the silver chain about her neck, ' 'tis nearly midnight! We shall have ample time in the future for such reminiscences, and on this occasion of all mustn't be late at the General Meeting!'

For it was no ordinary General Meeting they were due to attend, but one specially convened to present them with all the various gifts collected to mark the MPAS's appreciation of their past services.

'I must say it's a rum thought,' reflected Bernard, rising, 'that tonight's going to be our absolutely final appearance on the platform. I know everyone's going to miss seeing *you* there, Miss Bianca, and hearing you make your beautiful speeches!'

Miss Bianca accepted the compliment with a modest twitch of her whiskers. (Like her eyes and eyelashes they were dark brown. Her colouring, for a white mouse, was unusual altogether.) She still knew Bernard wasn't just flattering: 'Oohs' and 'Ahs' of admiration regularly greeted her every official appearance, whilst to listen to her famous silvery voice was considered by many Members as good as going to the Opera.

'All the same,' continued Bernard, opening the garden gate, 'what a lovely, peaceful, serene life you'll be able to lead now, Miss Bianca, just sitting in your Porcelain Pagoda writing poetry without a care in the world!'

'Except as to the reviews!' smiled Miss Bianca.

Actually her first slim volume of verse had gone into three editions, and that in preparation was already over-subscribed. When it is added that the Porcelain Pagoda was situated in the schoolroom of an Embassy, and that Miss Bianca was the Ambassador's son's particular friend (thus enjoying all diplomatic privileges), it will easily be seen that Bernard's total-peace-and-serenity forecast was soundly based.

But as another poet has observed, the best-laid schemes of mice and men gang aft a-gley.

In point of fact, Miss Bianca wasn't to mind them ganging a-gley nearly so much as Bernard did on her behalf. Miss Bianca, Bernard regretfully discovered, rather welcomed a brush, so to speak, with blood-hounds again. In the event it turned out to be a good deal more than a brush, and with creatures far larger, but meanwhile he escorted her to the Moot-house with a quiet mind.

2

The Moot-house, where all General Meetings of the MPAS took place, originated as an ancient claret-cask in the Embassy cellars; generations of mice had embellished it until it was as good as the Albert or Carnegie Hall. Neat match-box benches filled the body: upon the cigar-boxwood platform, chairs for the Committee were quite beautifully carpentered from walnut-shells. In front was a row of potted plants, and on the wall behind a richly-framed oil-painting depicting the famous incident of a mouse freeing a lion from a net, alongside a glass case containing such souvenirs of successful rescues as a map drawn by Miss Bianca and Nils's autograph in Norwegian.

For this particular occasion the Moot-house was naturally full to bursting. Children had to sit on their mothers' laps, there were standees not only at the back but in the aisles. Obviously the whole MPAS meant to make a big thing of the presentations! As Miss Bianca, on Bernard's arm, to even more than usual applause, ascended the platform, she beheld it heaped with a whole bazaar-ful of farewell gifts, and a whole queue of representative Members waiting to present them.

It may be said at once that all Bernard got was a stamp-album. Miss Bianca's tributes, almost too numerous and varied to detail, included a tea-cosy from the Ladies' Guild, a set of Emerson from the Mouse University Faculties, two dozen jars of jam from the MPAS Country-branch, and almost as many pin-cushions from the Orphanage: while for *pièce de résistance*, or *chef-d'oeuvre*, teetered a rocking-chair of bent matchwood offered by the MAHC (Mouse Arts and Handicrafts Centre).

Of course nothing could have been better intentioned, but when Miss Bianca's glance rested on that rocking-chair in particular, she really felt she was

not only retiring but being relegated to a Sunset
Home!

Of course, again, she let nothing of this appear in
her manner. She was too well bred. (A how-many-
times-great-great-grandmother had been that Blanche
de Versailles who cheered Marie Antionette in the
Conciergerie.) As each representative advanced to
present tea-cosy, jam-jar or what else, Miss Bianca
even let out little cries of pleasure and admiration.
At the gift from the MPAS Scout Troop she indeed
exclaimed quite spontaneously: it was a necklace of
teeth – their *own* teeth – neatly drilled and strung
together on a cat's whisker. 'We saved 'em every

time Ma slammed the oven door,' explained Shaun, the half-Irish troop-leader, who'd never forgotten a certain adventure with Miss Bianca involving, also rehabilitating, the whole outfit. 'That biggest in the middle's mine . . .' Behind him eleven more Scouts grinned gappily; what could Miss Bianca do but give the Scout left-hand grip to each and all?

So it went on, the atmosphere becoming more and more emotional, till Bernard gloomily foresaw they'd all end up singing 'Auld Lang Syne'. (This gloom on his part had nothing to do with getting only a stamp-album; he just saw Miss Bianca looking tired.) In fact Bernard had just made up his mind to cut the whole thing short and take her home, when who should appear, stumping up between the match-box benches, but Nils!

3

He was even more altered than Bernard or Miss Bianca. He had a wooden leg. But he still wore a sea-boot on the other, and with his striped woollen cap, and the cutlass through his belt, retained all his old air of nautical hardihood. The wooden leg just made him a bit more piratical-looking – and though his autograph was framed beside Miss Bianca's map, mice have such short memories, also such short lives, instead of welcoming him as a hero the assembly looked rather askance, if not (such is the irony of fate) downright disapproving.

Not so Bernard and Miss Bianca!

'Nils! My dear Nils!' cried Miss Bianca, warmly pressing his hands across the potted plants.

'Nils, you old beggar!' cried Bernard, knocking a geranium for six as he thumped him on the back.

'To think of your arriving in time for my farewell!' exclaimed Miss Bianca. 'I'm more touched than I can say! And how much we have to tell each other!'

'But not here,' added Bernard hastily. 'Let's get out of this crush and have a drink somewhere.'

'Certainly,' said Miss Bianca. 'At the Porcelain Pagoda Bernard shall open a bottle of my best claret!'

Miss Bianca had quite a cellar at the Pagoda. The Boy, the Ambassador's son, used to amuse himself by filling his mother's empty scent-bottles with any drops left over from an Embassy dinner-party. But as now the eye of Nils met the eye of Bernard, the message exchanged was Beer.

'If you could bring yourself to consider it, Miss Bianca,' said Bernard, 'my flat's quite a bit closer; and if Nils doesn't mind just Beer – '

'Not I!' said Nils heartily.

' – I could offer *you* a quite decent blackberry liqueur.'

'Indeed you make me feel quite adventurous again!' smiled Miss Bianca. (Never yet had she visited Bernard's bachelor apartment, but to have Nils as chaperon allayed all scruples.) 'Only wait while I make my personal adieux!'

Being Miss Bianca, she of course didn't hurry over them. Each representative donor – even the head-master of the Arts and Handicrafts Centre – went home feeling Miss Bianca especially delighted by a particular gift. It was thus with a clear social con-science that she at last crossed the threshold of Bernard's first-floor flat in the cigar-cabinet in the Ambassador's study – she and Bernard and Nils together, just like old times!

CHAPTER 2

Nils Again

Since the Ambassador gave up smoking, the empty cigar-cabinet was the best mouse-address going: most of the other tenants were doctors or lawyers. Its location had the further advantage that when the Ambassador wasn't at his desk, Bernard could easily nip up and take a look at his engagement-book. This wasn't just vulgar curiosity, but to give Miss Bianca notice if there was for instance a Banquet laid on (which meant she'd have to make a special toilet before attending it in the Boy's pocket), or if on the other hand a Shooting Party (from which the Boy was excluded, which meant she'd have to stay at home amusing him all day). Neither Miss Bianca nor Bernard on her behalf would have dreamed of intruding into the Ambassador's *private* diary — where indeed, if they *had*, they might have read the recurrent note, '*Still mice about . . .*'

(This being the very first time Miss Bianca had visited Bernard's bachelor apartment, obviously it wasn't she the Ambassador referred to. He wouldn't have minded Miss Bianca anyway. Both he and his wife the Ambassadress thoroughly appreciated her gentle, gay companionship of the Boy, their only child, who never did his lessons half so well as with her seated on his shoulder! Obviously the Ambassador meant the doctors and lawyers and so on.)

A happy mouse indeed was Bernard as Miss Bianca at last set foot upon, and whole-heartedly admired, his wall-to-wall stamp-paper carpeting, and then admired also the neat arrangement of his kitchen and clothes-closet and airing-cupboard — for he showed her all round straight away, even though Nils's tongue was practically hanging out. Then what a happy hour followed, as they all settled

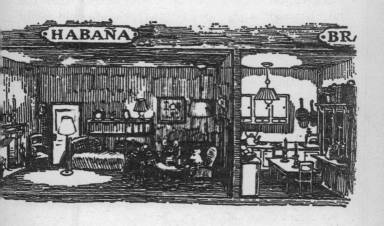

down in the sitting-room, Bernard and Nils knocking back beer, Miss Bianca sipping blackberry liqueur, exchanging all their news — Bernard and Miss Bianca of their adventures prisoner-rescuing, Nils of his adventures seafaring — how he'd lost his leg in a collision off Java, and shipped a new one in Hong Kong, and really found it much handier because it didn't need socks. It seemed he'd been half round the world since they last met, before fetching up in his home port of Oslo, when off he'd set again to see his old friends!

'And arriving so exactly in time for the Presentation Ceremonies!' marvelled Miss Bianca. 'My dear Nils, I'm more touched than I can say!'

Nils looked slightly abashed.

'Actually that was a bit of a lucky landfall,' he confessed. 'I was bound to come and see you anyway . . .'

It was at this moment that Bernard felt a first prickle of foreboding that the happy reunion might be going to end *un*.

'And quite time too!' chided Miss Bianca. 'Bernard and I were speaking of you only this evening!'

Nils took a gulp of beer. Bernard's beer was absolutely first-class. (He kept it ice-cold.) Even the froth emboldened, and Nils was on his second bottle. He still went a bit roundabout before revealing the true motive of his reappearance.

'You know what us Norwegians are, Miss Bianca,' said Nils, 'for getting into trouble. It seems to be a sort of Norwegian fate . . .'

'In my opinion, it's simply Norwegian carelessness,' said Bernard. 'We still don't know how that Poet of yours got himself into the Black Castle.'

'At any rate I can tell you how he's got himself into the Antarctic,' said Nils. 'He joined a scientific expedition.'

'How very praiseworthy!' said Miss Bianca interestedly. 'Science and poetry combined, the results should be rewarding indeed!'

'Only he's somehow got himself stuck there,' said Nils.

'He would,' said Bernard gloomily.

'You spoke of an Expedition,' interposed Miss Bianca. 'He didn't adventure into the Antarctic *alone*?'

'Well, no; to begin with there were five of 'em,' explained Nils. 'But the other four have all been lifted out by helicopter; it's only *our* chap that's somehow been left behind . . .'

'There you are,' said Bernard, 'sheer carelessness again! There'll just have to be another helicopter sent out.'

'Only the Air Ministry says it's too dangerous,' explained Nils. 'Of course I only know what I read in the papers; but with whirlwinds expected and ice-fields breaking up – here today and gone tomorrow – it seems it's too dangerous. Which is why,' finished Nils candidly, 'I thought of *you*, Miss Bianca!'

For a moment, in Bernard's sitting-room, total silence reigned. Though Nils's beer-mug was now empty, Bernard rather pointedly didn't open another bottle.

'It's a very sad tale,' said he. 'Very sad indeed; I think it's time I took Miss Bianca home.'

'It was bad enough for the poor chap in the Black Castle,' recalled Nils, 'totally imprisoned by stone walls and jailers and so on. *Now* he's totally imprisoned by ice. One of my own cousins was once trapped in a refrigerator; they carried him out stiff as a board.'

'As any mouse who doesn't know about refrigerators in this day and age deserves to be,' said Bernard. 'To which I'd add, any poet who doesn't know about the Antarctic. Are you ready, Miss Bianca?'

But though Miss Bianca rose – Bernard being her host, politeness impelled her – she also paused.

'What you relate, my dear Nils,' said she, 'touches us extremely. What more touching indeed, than loyalty to an old friend! Unless *faith* in old friends! But you see us no longer of any consequence in the MPAS. Both Bernard and I are retired.'

'I didn't say I thought of the MPAS,' reminded Nils stubbornly. 'I said I thought of *you*, Miss Bianca.'

To Bernard's dismay, Miss Bianca so to speak went on pausing.

'If there were anything I could do *personally* –' she began.

'Only there obviously isn't,' put in Bernard.

'Of course I only know what I read in the papers,' offered Nils again. 'It used to be just Movements of Shipping; but since the Poet took up exploration I've read the Scientific bits as well. Actually I read a whole piece about how from *these* parts a helicopter's sent up each week weather regardless, photographing from the air to make the first complete photographed maps of the Antarctic ever seen.'

Miss Bianca could well believe it. She knew the huge, powerful, rapacious country to which the Ambassador was accredited to be particularly interested in the Antarctic!

'So the thought just occurred to me,' ended Nils, looking into his empty beer-mug, which Bernard, again, made no motion to refill, 'that if someone who knew to watch out for the Poet went along, he might be rescued still. If it wasn't for this wooden leg you'd see *me* up in the rigging all right! But as it is I'd just be super-cargo. Which it seems I'm a bit of a one now,' added Nils, meeting Bernard's inhospitable eye, 'and if I don't nip down to the dock straight away, I may miss my passage home . . .'

'Then you'd better nip,' said Bernard, opening the front door and as soon as Nils had stumped through banging it shut again.

Let it not be thought that Bernard was heartless, in so brusquely dismissing an old comrade. It was just that he was so devoted to Miss Bianca, he couldn't bear the idea of any unrescued prisoner intruding upon and spoiling her total-peace-and-serenity retirement.

'What a good fellow he is!' said Bernard quite cordially (now that Nils was out of sight). 'How odd that we were speaking of him only this evening! Now I'll just take you home, Miss Bianca; and I can't say what a pleasure it's been to see you at last in my flat and really approving of the carpets.'

'*You* haven't a wooden leg,' observed Miss Bianca.

There was another pause. Bernard felt he could hardly mention his occasional touch of rheumatism.

'Nor I,' said Miss Bianca.

'I should hope not!' shuddered Bernard.

'In fact, for mice at retirement-age – the phrase I believe is Senior Citizens – we're both quite remarkably active,' reflected Miss Bianca.

Bernard couldn't deny it. Actually he no less than she had been struck by the inappropriateness of that rocking-chair. But he didn't mean to see her off adventuring again, not if he could help it!

Bernard wasn't a particularly clever mouse. He was brave, trustworthy, absolutely dependable upon in any jam, but not clever. Now, however, seeing Miss Bianca so obviously restless and disturbed by Nils's unfortunate reappearance, and proposals, he had a sudden clever idea.

How many times before hadn't he attempted to dissuade Miss Bianca from adventuring? And always with the result of making her more determined to? Though thoroughly admiring her innate heroism, Bernard had sometimes also suspected a streak of feminine contrariness; this time, he decided, he'd actually pretend to urge Miss Bianca on, trusting to that same contrariness to act in reverse.

'If you feel we *must* go after that feckless poetical ass, I suppose we must,' said Bernard.

'Dear Bernard, you read my thoughts!' exclaimed Miss Bianca joyfully.

'And agree with every one of 'em,' said Bernard. 'I dare say we'll *both* come back with wooden legs, but what of it?'

He was pleased to see Miss Bianca slightly shudder in turn.

'Frost-bite,' added Bernard musingly. 'I dare say we'll lose our ears as well. But again, what of it? Even if the Boy won't recognize you —'

'Not recognize me?' shuddered Miss Bianca. 'My own dear, dear Boy?'

'Well, not with a wooden leg and no ears,' said Bernard. It will be seen how cleverly he mingled persuasion with warning. Bernard had never felt so clever — indeed had never *been* so clever — in all his life. Miss Bianca was now positively shaking all over. Then she stopped.

' 'Twould be a true test of his affection for me indeed!' she smiled. 'Moreover I've just remembered something which can be called nothing less than an Omen!'

Bernard felt so put out and dejected, he could scarcely bring himself to ask What.

'Something you told me yourself!' added Miss Bianca teasingly.

Bernard just growled.

'When I asked you,' reminded Miss Bianca, 'to look in the Ambassador's diary and see if there were any banquet tonight — by this time, that is, *last* night — and you with your usual thoughtfulness for him said no, and a good thing too!'

'I haven't the faintest recollection,' said Bernard, though in fact one was beginning faintly to dawn, just as daylight was beginning faintly to dawn.

'Because today's first engagement is practically at sunrise,' reminded Miss Bianca, '*to see the helicopter off*. I dare say he's shaving already.'

Of course the Ambassador didn't normally get up at sunrise to witness a merely routine take-off, but Bernard's reviving memory now included a scribbled note alongside the engagement-entry, Memo: *take wreath*. The fact was that on this particular flight wreaths were to be dropped upon the patch of icy foam (or as near as the helicopter's captain could judge) wherein an ice-breaker and all its gallant crew had recently foundered. All Embassies were sending wreaths by Attachés, but the Boy's father intended going in person as a mark of extra respect. It was just this sort of thing that made him so popular and esteemed.

'And if *that* isn't an Omen, what is?' asked Miss Bianca triumphantly. 'The logistics of the operation I must admit rather baffled me, but now how all is simple! We just go along in the car and board the helicopter *by wreath*!'

In the face of such a thorough-going, everything-laid-on-Omen Bernard stopped trying to be clever and even as he growled a last growl began collecting a few necessaries such as a tin-opener and a box of cough-lozenges, to tie up in the big spotted handkerchief that served him as travelling carry-all.

'Dear Bernard, I felt your enthusiasm from the

AVE
ATQUE
VALE

first!' smiled Miss Bianca. 'Now where do you suppose is Nils?'

3

Actually when Bernard opened the door, there was Nils just outside.

He'd made himself quite comfortable, his wooden leg propped between the banisters, his shoulders against a laundry-box Bernard had forgotten to take in. He didn't exactly wink at Miss Bianca, as she and Bernard emerged; his left eyelid just flickered. Nor did he make any conventional excuse about being so tired after his journeyings he'd just dropped off to

sleep. The three friends knew each other so well, Bernard no less than Miss Bianca saw at once that Nils had never really believed they'd disappoint him, and even Bernard was now glad they hadn't. Cutting all corners,

'First by car, then by wreath,' said Miss Bianca briskly. 'If you'd care to come and see us off, that is, without missing your passage home – ?'

'I'd miss my passage to the Last Harbour!' declared Nils fervently.

'Then I'll just run up to the Pagoda,' said Miss Bianca, 'for my overnight bag.'

While Bernard escorted her – he never liked Miss Bianca going anywhere by daylight alone – Nils promised to lock up the flat, not forgetting to take the laundry in, before they met at the car.

'Dash it!' said Bernard, a moment later in the schoolroom, 'I should have told him to leave a note for the milkman as well!'

Miss Bianca, overnight bag in hand (of snail-tortoiseshell lined with spider-silk, containing chiefly a brush and a bottle of eau de cologne), paused.

'So should I perhaps leave a note for the Boy,' said she, 'or he may worry at my absence? Have I time?'

'No,' said Bernard firmly. 'We shan't be gone more than a day or two.' (He was always a bit jealous of the Boy. He couldn't help it. Also *he*'d sometimes had to worry about Miss Bianca for whole weeks.) 'No,' repeated Bernard, 'and never mind the milkman either. If we don't make haste, we may be left behind!'

'Well, if it's only for a day or two – !' agreed Miss Bianca.

What was it the poet Burns said?

CHAPTER 3

Up and Away!

Immediately, however, all went as smoothly as possible. Bernard and Nils and Miss Bianca sat beside the chauffeur, or rather in the big laurel-wreath propped at his left elbow. (The car had a right-hand drive.) The close-set leaves afforded splendid camouflage, which Miss Bianca felt just as well, since though she knew the Ambassador's chauffeur to be remarkably steady, the unexpected appearance of three mice, one with a wooden leg, might well have surprised him to the point of having an accident. Actually the chauffeur did glimpse and recognize Miss Bianca's ermine coat, but being a close friend of the Boy's knew she shared all diplomatic privileges, and thought she'd just come for the ride. Across the breadth of the wreath was looped a wide black ribbon lettered in gold with the words AVE ATQUE VALE, which Miss Bianca, since the Boy did Latin, was easily able to translate as HAIL AND FARE-WELL. She also introduced her companions to several other handy phrases in that universal tongue, such as *Magna Est Veritas* (Great is Truth), and *Cave Canem* (Beware of the Dog): and in fact led quite a cultural conversation ere Bernard suddenly remarked that they were on the point of being unloaded.

'Nip down while you can!' he adjured Nils.

Nils nipped. Only Miss Bianca and Bernard still

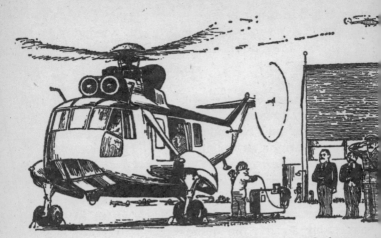

clung to the garland as up by willing hands it was lofted into the helicopter. 'The luck of the mice go with you!' shouted Nils, as the Ambassador stood to attention. Then up rose the big whirly-bird and clattered away on its course due South.

2

There were half a dozen other wreaths on board, all save one also of laurel – it was obviously the general idea. The odd-one-out was composed of chrysanthemums, red and white in alternate chunks, the big solid flowerheads so closely packed, the effect was more of a life-belt than a floral tribute, which Miss Bianca, in the circumstances, found slightly *macabre*. Fond of flowers as she was, she greatly preferred the plain laurel leaves! One thing absolutely every

32

wreath had in common, however, was the legend on its ribbon : AVE ATQUE VALE. Miss Bianca was pleased to see her point about Latin-the-universal-language so swiftly illustrated; on the other hand, it made for rather monotonous reading-matter. However, all wreaths were ditched as soon as possible.

'Too much top-hamper aboard altogether!' decided the helicopter's Captain. 'I feel as though I'm flying a blooming greenhouse! Would you say,' he asked his Navigator, 'we're anywhere near or nearabouts the tragic spot?'

'At any rate nearabouts,' replied the Navigator. 'Also what with tides and currents and so on, I'd call almost anywhere now near enough.'

'I don't want to show lack of respect,' said the Captain.

'Actually the skipper of that ice-breaker was an uncle of mine,' said the Navigator, 'and I know what *he*'d do with any top-hamper.'

'Then over they go,' decided the Captain; and out through the hatch went the lot, leaving the craft indeed much more shipshape.

There were six aboard altogether, not counting mice : the crew, consisting of the Captain, or pilot, his Navigator and a Mechanic; plus a Photographer, a Hydrographer (which means someone who makes maps of the sea), and a Fisheries-expert whose job it was to spot and add up seals because a full-grown seal consumes about a hundred pounds of fish a day. All were so fully preoccupied, especially as the great land-mass of the Antarctic loomed below at last, Miss Bianca uneasily recognized that the only means of directing anyone's attention to a poet would have to be by exceptionally powerful thought-transference.

Luckily it was something she was exceptionally good at. How often, seated on the Boy's shoulder in the Embassy schoolroom, had she not thought-transferred to him the right answer to some hard question from his Tutor! So it wasn't surprising that after being concentrated on by Miss Bianca for several hours the Captain suddenly observed that he seemed to remember something about a chap being left behind from the Norwegian expedition recently returned to Norway.

'Might as well keep an eye out for him too!' said the Captain to the Fisheries-expert.

Up and along, then dipping down, then up and along again flew the big whirly-bird. Miss Bianca felt a great sympathy with it – it was so much more bird-like than any of the jets she was accustomed to travel in! She still didn't attempt any thought-transference *there* – she knew too little about machinery; it was the Captain's initiative that suddenly dipped the craft lower than ever before, above a sort of peak sticking out from the snow, alongside which lay a long, rough-hairy shape . . .

'A big bull-seal, would you say?' he asked the Fisheries-expert.

'Could be,' said the Expert, like all experts hedging. 'On the other hand, no sufficient brachial development (by which he meant humpiness about the shoulders) to make identification certain . . .'

'Might even be a chap?' suggested the Captain

(and Miss Bianca). 'I'm certainly not going to land here, it's too risky; but lower the winch and see if there's any reaction.'

'Lower me with it, sir, just to make sure,' proposed the Mechanic, who was longing to distinguish himself on account of a girl at home.

'Too risky,' repeated the Captain. 'It's a gallant offer, my gallant lad, but all crew stays strictly aboard!'

Of course in the circumstances he was right, and a Captain's word is law. But equally of course he had no authority over mice, and the moment the line began to drop Miss Bianca, overnight bag in hand, closely followed by Bernard clutching his handkerchief, ran down and made ready to jump off.

3

Luckily again it was only a few inches from the last dangling loop, and no more than a few yards (so accurately had the Captain manœuvred) to the recumbent form not of any seal but of the Poet indeed! – huddled in half-frozen, half-deathly sleep, one mittened hand still clasping the Complete Works of Shakespeare, Leopold Edition.

'It's him all right!' panted Bernard.

'We must rouse him, and immediately!' cried Miss Bianca. 'If necessary, bite!'

Bernard was just about to observe that through such thick furry garments as enabled a poet to be mistaken for a seal, no bite of mouse could possibly penetrate, when the Poet himself spontaneously stirred and staggered to his feet. No doubt it was the noise of the helicopter that had waked him; he still didn't seem properly aware of its gladsome presence. He rose, and then staggered a step or two, but as it were blindly . . .

'Follow *us*!' shrieked Miss Bianca. 'Follow me, Miss Bianca, and Bernard! Have we not guided you to safety once before?'

She ran back towards the dangling line. Whether or not he properly heard her, the Poet at least stumbled in the right direction – and there could be no mis-hearing the Captain's loud encouragement through a megaphone! 'TAKE HOLD AND HANG ON!' shouted the Captain. With a sudden burst of still only-partly-conscious energy – catching indeed at a *life*-line! – the Poet did so. Bernard and Miss Bianca were only seconds behind – yet still, as the hoist jerked up, too late!

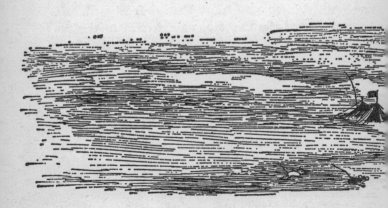

Mice (indeed like everyone else) are always better at jumping *down* than *up* . . .

In short, while the Poet was winched to safety, Bernard and Miss Bianca *were left behind*!

CHAPTER 4

Alone in the Antarctic!

For a moment, as the full awfulness of their situation dawned, neither spoke. They couldn't. The only sound to break the huge, fearsome, all-encompassing Antarctic silence was the clatter of the helicopter whirling up and away. Only as it finally disappeared –

'At least we may consider our mission successfully accomplished!' said Miss Bianca. 'At least the *Poet* is rescued!'

'Only who's going to rescue *us*?' enquired Bernard grimly. 'I tell you frankly, Miss Bianca, I don't believe even you and I have ever been in such dire peril! For who knows even where we are, except Nils, probably at sea again till the cows come home? Even five more minutes of this and we'll both be found stiff as boards just like his cousin in the refrigerator. In fact a refrigerator's exactly what we're in – the ice-cube part.'

Truth to tell, Miss Bianca in her heart was equally appalled by their peril's direness. But she knew better than Bernard how to disguise her feelings, also had looked about more, and twitched her whiskers encouragingly.

'Doubtless you are perfectly right,' said she, 'except that I for one don't intend to be found looking like Nils's deplorable relation. We must therefore gain some sort of shelter without delay, and see, it could hardly lie closer!'

So speaking, she indicated the Complete Works of Shakespeare dropped from the Poet's frozen mitt as he clutched at the helicopter-line. Fallen spine-up and half open, it looked just like a tent, and just mouse-size! Moreover its 1000-odd pages, as Miss Bianca and Bernard discovered as soon as they ran in, afforded quite splendid insulation. However bleak the Antarctic wastes without, inside the Complete Works of Shakespeare it was positively snug. There was even a carpet, if rather narrow, in the shape of the Poet's soft leather bookmark embossed with Art Nouveau daisies; whilst a further happy circum-

stance was that where the volume had opened, between pages 560 and 561, was in the middle of *Twelfth Night*, Miss Bianca's favourite play and so of course Bernard's as well.

Nothing so composes the mind in peril as a little good reading, and the print of the Leopold Edition was just mouse-size too.

'*Most excellent, accomplished lady, the heavens*
 rain odours on you!'
read Bernard, off page 560 – and feeling glad indeed that Miss Bianca had her eau de cologne with her.

'*I can no other answer make but thanks,*'
read Miss Bianca off page 561.

'*And thanks, and ever thanks . . .*'
'*Why then methinks 'tis time to smile again!*'
read Bernard off page 560.

They didn't read much more because both were so tired they turned in – Bernard between pages 552/3, Miss Bianca between 566/7. She still just managed to compose a grateful quatrain, or four-line verse, ere slumber overtook her quite.

QUATRAIN COMPOSED BY
MISS BIANCA PRACTICALLY IN HER SLEEP

O Bard of Avon! 'Neath thy sheltering wings
 (*Or pages printed with immortal verse*),
Behold a true admirer of thine art
 Preserved from death by freezing, if not worse!
                    M. B.

Actually she didn't expect anything really worse than freezing, nor was the rhyme quite true; but in the circumstances it might have been a great deal worser verse, as anyone conversant with verse must agree.

2

Though they were for the moment positively snug, Bernard's first feeling of grimness was nonetheless justified. All about their tiny shelter stretched the huge, bleak, pitiless Antarctic: only Nils, that vagabond of the seas, knew where they'd gone. The MPAS didn't know, nor the Boy; as for the Poet, it was Bernard's strong impression that he hadn't recognized even Miss Bianca, ere stumbling blindly towards the helicopter that rescued *him* all right . . .

'I'll still get you back too, Miss Bianca,' promised Bernard (practically in *his* sleep), 'to the elegant security and retirement of your Porcelain Pagoda!'

Of course he couldn't (practically in his sleep) be expected to think exactly *how*!

3

How long they both went on sleeping they didn't know, for neither Bernard nor Miss Bianca carried a watch. They were used to just looking at the clock in whatever room where they happened to be; and since in the Antarctic there weren't even rooms, there were naturally no Grandfathers or Cuckoos to consult either. But at least they must have slept through a whole long Antarctic night, for when they woke it was just beginning to be daylight again, and both were so sufficiently refreshed as to feel hungry.

Actually Bernard woke (first) so extremely hungry, before Miss Bianca roused in turn he'd explored as far back as page 490 to see if there were any crumb or candle-drip (such as he'd often found in books before) left pressed between the leaves. But of course the Poet had been too careful and respectful : there wasn't so much as a greasy finger-print as far back as *The Merry Wives of Windsor*.

'I believe some chaps can live on poetry alone,' remarked Bernard to Miss Bianca, as soon as she too was up, 'but I'm dashed if *I* can . . .'

'I doubt whether even the Poet could !' smiled Miss Bianca. She looked quite her elegant self : while Bernard was nosing between pages 547/481 she'd made almost a usual toilet – fur brushed with eau de cologne, tail and whiskers similarly sleeked. (Bernard, taking a dekko outside at page 498, had taken also an involuntary shower under a dollop of ice melting from the Leopold Edition's eaves. Fortunately mice dry very quickly, and now his coat was only staring.) 'I doubt whether even the Poet would !' said Miss Bianca. 'In fact I'm sure he couldn't. Within that larger tent beside which we first observed him I shouldn't be surprised to find all sorts of provisions ! Moreover 'tis quite close at hand,' she added, slipping out at page 560 to take a dekko herself, 'so why not to breakfast at once?'

From the Leopold Edition (call it, in explorers' parlance, Camp One) to the Expedition's hut (call it Camp Two) was indeed scarcely more than a few yards: but no sooner had they begun the short transit, Miss Bianca slightly in the lead, when to Bernard's horror she totally disappeared!

4

It wasn't any magic; it was simply that her pure white coat merged so completely in the universal, all-surrounding whiteness. Bernard himself, brown all over, was conspicuous as a raisin in a milk-pudding, but only Miss Bianca's huge dark eyes, fringed by long dark lashes, and her long dark whiskers, made her visible at all. From behind, even her whisker-tips disappeared, they were so delicate!

'Where are you, Miss Bianca?' yelled Bernard desperately, not daring to move. 'Do pray come back!'

Miss Bianca turned in surprise. Of course as soon as she did so Bernard could see her again, and as the explanation dawned he explained it back to Miss Bianca to explain his otherwise inexplicable outburst.

'I'm sure you relieve me greatly!' said she. 'For a moment I feared you smitten with snow-blindness!'

Bernard, though equally relieved to know that *that* wasn't the explanation, still halted uneasily.

'Perhaps we'd better be roped together?' he suggested.

'My dear Bernard, we aren't *mountaineering*!' exclaimed Miss Bianca. 'In fact I've never seen such general flatness!'

(It may be said at once that Bernard's and Miss Bianca's experience of the huge, cruel Antarctic was to be narrow enough. They were to know nothing – their legs were too short – of its awful, towering mountains such as Mount Erebus. Bernard's and Miss Bianca's total experience of the Antarctic was contained within a mere acre or so, and that offered dangers enough!)

'It's just that you disappear so,' persisted Bernard unhappily. 'I know it's a lot to ask, Miss Bianca, but if you could possibly bring yourself to wear my handkerchief round your neck – '

Miss Bianca frowned. She had long disapproved of Bernard's attachment to his big blue-and-red spotted handkerchief. For months – by mouse-calendar, for years – she'd been urging him to buy a proper briefcase. She nonetheless saw his point: against the all-surrounding whiteness the horrid object would certainly *show up*!

'It's quite clean,' pressed Bernard. 'It goes to the laundry like clockwork, and all that's in it now is a box of cough-lozenges and a tin-opener and an odd piece of string or two!'

Miss Bianca was quite touched to see how eagerly he emptied all these useful articles out upon the snow. Also her instinct for personal elegance had

gone by the board often enough before, in the interests of prisoner-rescuing; hadn't she once tied her own cobweb scarf over her ears in the likeness of a yashmak? So after but a moment's more hesitation she accepted to let Bernard tie on his handkerchief.

It was so large, in proportion to her slight frame, she had to wear it rather as a shawl.

'That's better!' said Bernard thankfully. 'And I do assure you, Miss Bianca, it's most becoming! You look just as though you were going to one of the Embassy Fancy-balls dressed as a village maiden.'

'I only hope no village maiden ever finds herself in such a situation as *this*!' responded Miss Bianca a trifle tartly – also for once rather unfairly, the whole enterprise being quite as much, or even more, due to her own initiative as to Bernard's. But the handkerchief smelled so strongly of cough-lozenges, while besides eau de cologne all she cared for was a touch of rose-water. 'May we now *proceed*,' added Miss Bianca, still rather tartly, 'in the hope of breaking our fast?'

'You bet!' said Bernard. He was actually the hungrier, also knew from experience that whatever happens *after* breakfast is never so dismaying as what happens to have happened *before*.

At least such had been his experience hitherto . . .

CHAPTER 5

Camp Two

What most struck Miss Bianca, as they entered Camp Two, was the pathos of the five empty, discarded sleeping-bags. What most struck Bernard was the quantity of grub left about.

There were heel-ends of packets of oatmeal and raisins, any number of banana-skins, jars of honey and molasses with their lids off – these to be sure mostly empty – and besides all else, quite untouched, an enormous red, round Dutch cheese.

It was as big and round and red and shiny as a setting sun, and to Bernard at least quite as beautiful.

'What a whopper!' breathed Bernard, so lost in admiration he momentarily forgot how hungry he was. 'And what a wonderfully rich patina!' ('Patina' was a word he'd learnt from Miss Bianca on the occasion when she showed him over the Embassy drawing-room, and is usually employed to describe the lustre on antique furniture and *objets d'art*. Bernard was delighted to find an opportunity to employ it himself, especially on so much worthier an *objet*.) 'Why, we could live on it for weeks and weeks!' he added enthusiastically. 'May I nibble you a bit now, Miss Bianca?'

Miss Bianca, however, opted for raisin-and-honey, and Bernard, admiring her delicate taste, was in and out of a raisin-packet in two shakes; then he turned to the honey-jars to see which one had most traces of honey left under the rim, and was just about to roll it over (as a room-waiter wheels in a trolley), when something struck him.

'There seem to be an awful lot of footprints around here,' remarked Bernard. 'Or even *paw-prints* . . .'

Now that Miss Bianca looked too, she did indeed observe, where the snow had drifted in, a number of broad, puggy slots, definitely thicker around the honey-jars than anywhere else.

'You don't think it's polar bears?' suggested Bernard uneasily.

'No,' said Miss Bianca. 'This isn't the *Arctic*, my dear Bernard, but the *Ant*, where there are positively no polar bears at all. Doubtless the explorers, when they came in, took off their boots and put on moccasins, which accounts for the shape.'

Bernard never minded being corrected by Miss Bianca, especially when as now she so relieved his mind. As she delicately wiped a trace of honey on her raisin, Bernard addressed himself to a banana-skin with all the undivided attention it proved to deserve. Even allowing for his appetite, he'd never in his life tasted anything so succulent and aromatic and toothsome and satisfying, let alone tender and flavoursome and perfectly brought to table.

'Do just taste, Miss Bianca,' urged Bernard. 'It's absolutely *black*!'

For blackness, in a banana-skin, is as much prized by mice as is blackness in caviare by their elders if not betters. It was always the black caviare, not the

inferior red variety, that the Ambassadress served at
her dinner-parties. Nothing loath, since she too was
hungrier than usual, Miss Bianca accepted to nibble
at the banana's other end. But well ere she was
replete (and Bernard even less so), she, just as he had,
paused.

'Not a nibble more,' declared Miss Bianca firmly,
'of this excellent, black, *pliant* banana-skin!'

'Why ever not?' asked Bernard in surprise.
'There's dozens and dozens!'

'Of which we shall need every one,' said Miss

Bianca seriously. 'Think, my dear Bernard: as you yourself so pertinently enquired, who is to rescue *us*, our whereabouts so completely unknown? We must therefore set about rescuing *ourselves*, and don't you remember how useful that SOS turned out, that I sowed with mustard-and-cress in the Orient?'

Indeed Bernard remembered. How otherwise should he and she have survived to risk freezing to death in the Antarctic?

'Even if we'd the seeds, which we haven't,' still objected Bernard, 'I doubt whether they'd sprout *here*. Or if you're thinking of tramping out the letters in the snow, though I know my feet are the biggest in the whole MPAS – ' Bernard was always sensitive about the size of his feet – 'the helicopter, if that's what you're thinking of, wouldn't ever notice in weeks.'

'You meet my thought exactly,' said Miss Bianca. 'Which is where these I must admit quite delicious banana-skins come in. An SOS in *black*, upon snow and ice, must almost certainly attract notice! Therefore let us at once seek some appropriate flat surface and set to work!'

With which words, she rose. So did Bernard. One of Bernard's many good qualities was that he could always see reason, and he now accepted Miss Bianca's reasonable plan so whole-heartedly, he there and then (after but a last nibble) began hauling on the banana-skin. However, when Miss Bianca pointed out that it would probably save time in the end if they just trod out the letters first, he wasn't sorry to let go, because it weighed like a ton. Of course he was ready to haul till he dropped when the time arrived, but perhaps hoped for a second nibble ere.

2

Just behind Camp Two Bernard and Miss Bianca discovered the very terrain they sought – an area about the size of a tennis-court, flat as a pancake, evenly crusted with snow white as the best icing-sugar. Miss Bianca's and Bernard's footprints, as they embarked respectively on the S and O, took like fork-prongs on piecrust.

For some moments each stepped in concentrated silence. Then –

'How very odd!' said Miss Bianca, looking up from the curve of the S. 'I don't seem to remember that *hillock*! It must be drifting snow : in fact a snow-drift . . .'

'Over here there's another,' said Bernard, half-way down the O. 'And much bigger; really quite enor-mous! I say, Miss Bianca, the snow must drift pretty fast round here!'

'No doubt owing to the prevailing winds,' said Miss Bianca. 'And truly how beautiful, what a wel-come break in the flatness, so beautifully large and rounded a hillock as *yours*!'

Seeing her so appreciative, Bernard gazed apprecia-tively too, as he always did when Miss Bianca tried to make him appreciate the beauties of nature. Of his own accord he'd once managed to appreciate the

52

surface of a lake as reminding him of the top of a tin of tongue; now he spontaneously observed that the shape of the bigger snow-drift reminded him of the picture of a polar bear on a frozen-fish-finger carton.

In fact it reminded him so very vividly, he couldn't help harking back even at the risk of being corrected again.

'Unless it really *is* a polar bear?' suggested Bernard.

'Of course not,' said Miss Bianca. 'Didn't I tell you that in the Antarctic they don't exist?'

The words were scarcely out of her mouth when down on either side – hemming her in, absolutely impeding any further progress on the S – plumped the fore-paws of an unmistakable large-as-life polar bear cub!

'Look, Ma!' squealed he excitedly. 'I've caught a Fairy!'

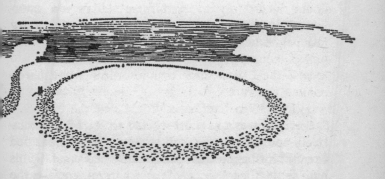

CHAPTER 6

An Extraordinary Encounter

The big mother-bear, who had just lolled down for a nap north of Bernard's O, opened one eye.

'Nonsense, my love,' said she, in a voice that sounded like a sort of kindly thunder – that is, big and booming, and deep and powerful, but not frightening. 'Fairies are only in fairy-tales . . .'

'But it *is*,' persisted the cub, beginning to pat up a little ring-wall of snow so that Miss Bianca shouldn't escape. (At the moment she could have climbed out quite easily, but was too indignant, so to speak, with the circumstances to take advantage of them. Bernard, inches away on the O, ran in to be beside her.)

'Nonsensical as *my* presence may seem to your parent,' said Miss Bianca, indignantly, 'hers (and yours) is certainly no less bizarre! Don't you know you're at the wrong Pole altogether? If you have any rational explanation, I shall be glad, though surprised, to hear it!'

'Ma, the Fairy wants to know how we're here,' relayed the cub.

'Why, on an Exchange Visit!' said the big bear. She herself was too short-sighted to see Miss Bianca at all, and thought her son was just making up. But like all sensible mothers she didn't equate making up with telling lies, just saw it as a natural exercise for youthful brains. 'An Exchange Visit,' she repeated instructively, 'with a Committee of seals; seals know nearly as much about cold-water fishing as we polar bears!'

'*I* think the Fairy means how did we get here?' persisted the cub.

'No ocean is too deep, no distance too great, for polar bears – and in fact for seals as well – to take in their swim on any matter of importance,' said his mother. 'Always remember that, my love, if ever you're in such a position of importance as your father!'

'And did *I* swim all those miles and miles?' asked the cub eagerly.

'Well, in a way,' smiled his mother. 'Let's say *I* did the swimming; but you were certainly here in time to be born!'

Of course Bernard and Miss Bianca overheard the whole conversation, and Bernard was so glad to find he hadn't boobed, and Miss Bianca, after her initial disapproval, was so interested by the idea of Exchange Visits, neither paid attention to the cub all the time patting the ring-wall higher.

'Look, Ma!' he squealed. 'I've built a whole snow-castle for my Fairy!'

So he had. The ring-wall towered like battlements, while outside, where he'd scooped, was a proper moat. Neither Bernard nor Miss Bianca could run out easily now . . .

'So you have, my clever little son!' said his mother, without really looking, as mothers some-times don't when wanting to get back to a nap.

'And may I keep her?' begged the cub.

'So long as you don't get too upset when she vanishes!' said the big bear.

All mothers, of whatever shape or weight, are aware of this hazard in allowing their offspring to keep pets – from hamsters to puppy-dogs through goldfish and lizards . . .

'And so long as you remember to feed her!' added the big bear, who though she still imagined Miss Bianca to be imaginary saw a chance to teach her cub responsibility.

'That I will!' promised the cub. 'What do Fairies eat, Ma?'

'Why, all that is rarest!' smiled his mother, dropping back into a snooze.

2

All that was rarest (in the way of food) meant to the cub all the scraps and bottoms of packets and jars left behind in the Norwegian expedition's tent. It was his paw-marks that lay so thick about the honey-jars, his greedy tongue that had licked round and round inside. So back to that deserted larder he trotted, and pitched upon as rarest food of all the big, round, red, untouched Dutch cheese.

It was so extremely large and red and round and important-looking he hadn't yet given it a bite in case it bit back. (He was a very young cub.) But now for the sake of his Fairy he bravely trundled it out between his fore-paws, and all the way back to the snow-castle battlements, and sent it rolling over them like a cannon-ball. The mice dodged just in time.

'Good-oh!' cried Bernard impulsively, as soon as he saw Miss Bianca hadn't been squashed. 'That cub's

not a bad little chap after all! As I said before, we can live on that beautiful cheese for weeks and weeks!'

'I trust we may not need to,' said Miss Bianca. 'The fact remains, however, that as once we were imprisoned in a Black Castle, so now we seem to be imprisoned in a white . . .'

3

'Twas only too true. There was even a moat.

'I'm afraid you're right,' admitted Bernard.

'We must therefore attempt to escape ere that

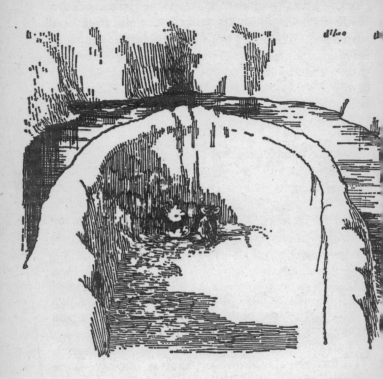

good little chap builds even higher!' said Miss Bianca, with restraint.

Bernard could only admit her right again; so as soon as the cub and his mother went home for lunch (the cub promising to be back first thing next day), Bernard and Miss Bianca attempted till they ached in every limb.

As is well known, mice can run up almost anything – Hickory-dickory-dock, a mouse ran up a clock — but the snowflaky interior surface of the castle walls crumbled into particles under even Bernard's and Miss Bianca's minuscule weight: the most Bernard achieved was about three inches before he came tumbling back, and Miss Bianca (half his size) barely four ere she more elegantly glissaded, but still *back* . . .

So it always happened during the days to come as well, for Bernard never knew when he was beat, and Miss Bianca's outward fragility deceived; but though never a day passed without their attempting the battlements afresh, it always ended in frustration. The best point about the castle was that with so much soft feathery snow slipping down, whenever Miss Bianca sank exhausted a little natural sofa or chaise-longue at once formed beneath her form, and wherever Bernard flopped he was practically in a sleeping-bag. (Again, it was the difference in their weights.) They also had ample provision of cheese to eat and ice-water for drinking. In fact Bernard and Miss Bianca might have fared far worse in the cruel Antarctic, save that they were jailed there!

POEM BY MISS BIANCA FACING THE FACT

Stone walls do not a prison make,
  Nor iron bars a cage,
At least so said a poet once,
  In some far-distant age.
'Tis all too plain he did not know
Of walls of snow.

Once more into the breach, dear friends!
  A greater poet wrote.
Would that dear friends could breach indeed
  These walls above the moat!
Alas, they do not even know
Us jailed in snow!

M. B.

CHAPTER 7

Humbert

Miss Bianca herself admitted they could have had
no more kindly jailer than the polar bear, whose
name he told them was Humbert. In fact he quite
reminded her of the big white Persian cat (pet of the
Ambassadress) ever welcome in the schoolroom for
his affability and good-breeding.* Humbert wasn't
even much larger, and in colouring would have been
identical, save that his eyes and nose, instead of
golden, were black as blackberries. His eyes were
also un-Persianly small – indeed anyone less poetic-
ally inclined than Miss Bianca might have likened
them not to blackberries but to boot-buttons. In any
case, whenever they rested on his Fairies, boot-
buttons or blackberries brimmed with affection . . .

As soon as he noticed Bernard, Humbert decided
that Bernard must be a Fairy too, but without paying
him particular attention. Bernard for his part was
used to being rather overlooked, when in company
with Miss Bianca, and bore no grudge.

Each morning, down trotted Humbert to his snow-
castle, patted up a fresh battlement or two, then
pushed his blackberry-nose between the latest towers
and asked Miss Bianca to tell him fairy-tales.

Rather to the latter's surprise, he seemed to know

* This explains why Miss Bianca wasn't afraid of cats. See
The Rescuers.

most of them already, yet with interesting varia-
tions. *Goldilocks and the Three Bears*, naturally his
favourite, had for heroine not a little girl but a little
seal : (instead of 'Who's been sleeping in *my* bed?'
'Who's been fishing in *my* pool?'). Another little
seal, evidently Cinderella, after being bullied by all
her relations married the eldest son of the King of
the Northern Lights, and so became Princess Aurora
Borealis. If Aladdin had his wonderful lamp, a lucky
penguin had a magic pebble; while as for Ali Baba
and the Forty Thieves, Humbert identified them at
once with a shoal of forty killer sharks outwitted by
a clever mermaid, who for *her* reward was taken up
into the Zodiac!

In fact Miss Bianca was driven to making up quite
new fairy-stories, and one in particular was so successful, it seems a pity not to give it.

THE THREE LOVING BROTHERS

'Once upon a time — ' began Miss Bianca.

'*Ma* begins, Once in the Ice-age,' interrupted
Humbert.

'Shush!' said Bernard.

'Once upon a time,' repeated Miss Bianca firmly,
'there lived in the Antarctic three loving brothers.'
(She had no need to tell Humbert they were polar
bears; he took it for granted.) 'Their names were Ice,
Frost and Snow, and they were orphans; but by
always snuggling together for warmth, and always
sharing whatever fish any one of them could catch,
they grew up to be so big and strong, everyone
admired and respected them. Each could have asked

for anyone's fair daughter's hand in marriage and not been refused; only they never did, because each in his secret heart — (their hearts naturally beat as one) — dreamed of marrying a mermaid . . .'

'Wouldn't *I* like to marry a mermaid!' squealed Humbert, wriggling with excitement.

Bernard shushed him again.

'So every night,' continued Miss Bianca, 'they went down to the beach to hear the mermaids sing; of whom three in particular, named Coral, Pearl and Anemone, often happened to be closest in-shore; and also had the sweetest voices and the longest green-gold hair which they combed with their tortoiseshell combs. In fact, to make matters short — '

'I don't want it to be *short*!' cried Humbert.

''Twill be quite long enough!' promised Miss Bianca. 'As long as a mermaid's hair! To come to the point, let us say then, the three brothers soon discovered they didn't want to marry simply *any* mermaid, but specifically Coral and Anemone and Pearl. Frost wanted to marry Coral, and Ice Anemone, and Snow Pearl, and as soon as this was sorted out they proposed straight away.

'The three mermaids put their heads together and giggled. Then they whispered.

' "We like you very much!" said Coral at last. "In fact we like you better than any merman, or dolphin, or swordfish we've ever seen! But we have long decided that ere we marry, we must each receive as a wedding gift the rarest object on land or sea."

' "Done!" cried Frost.

' "Never fear!" promised Snow.

' "What is it?" asked Ice.

' "A roc's egg!" cried all the mermaids together.'
('They never!' squealed Humbert, quite appalled.)

'Here was a test indeed,' continued Miss Bianca,
'for as I see Humbert at least is aware, never more
than one pair of rocs breed at a time, and never lay
more than three eggs at a clutch: moreover with
their sharp beaks and cruel talons defend their
property to the last feather. However, off the
brothers set – '

Here it was Bernard who interrupted.

'How often haven't I heard you tell the Boy, Miss
Bianca, bird-nesting's wrong?' interrupted Bernard.
'Especially if of a rare species?'

'Rocs are not only rare, they're mythological,'

retorted Miss Bianca, which meant this was only a story after all. 'So off the three brothers set, and after a most desperate climb up to the rocs' mountain-top eyrie, and then after a most desperate mountain-top battle during which their eyes were almost plucked out and great tufts of their fur *quite*, victory was at last in their grasp when the furious rocs, sooner than admit defeat, themselves rolled out two of the eggs to be smashed on the stones below! So the brothers had only one egg to take back between them.'

'Whatever did they do then?' gasped Humbert.

'They took it down to the sea-shore,' said Miss Bianca, 'and while waiting for the mermaids to appear, discussed the situation.'

' "Of course it's Ice's," said Frost to Snow. "Ice did the worst of the fighting."

' "So he did,' agreed Snow. "Though I must say *you*'ve lost most hair!"

' "Anyway he's the eldest and biggest," said Frost.

' "Stop a moment," said Ice. "Look at all the scratches on Snowy's nose! Considering he's the youngest and smallest, wasn't he the bravest? In my opinion it's Snow who deserves the egg to win a bride with, and you and I must just put up with being bachelors." '

'Oh, *no*!' begged Humbert. 'I don't want them to!'

'At which moment,' continued Miss Bianca, 'up from the hollow of a wave, where they'd been listening all the time, popped Coral and Anemone and Pearl.

' "Don't bother about that old egg a minute

more!" cried Coral. "Haven't you each brought us a far rarer present still, a truly loving and loyal and unselfish heart?"'

Though hardly comprehending their good fortune (so Miss Bianca described the joyful scene), the three brothers with a simultaneous *whoosh* hit the billow. Light as spray, a mermaid mounted each poor plucked-about back and steered for the court of the King of the Sea, sometimes known as Neptune, who married them all straight off and they lived happy ever after.

Humbert liked this story so much, he made Miss Bianca tell it again and again. When he knew it by heart he repeated it to his mother, who in turn, after she was back home from the Exchange Visit, often told it to kindergartens in the Arctic.

So perhaps Miss Bianca added one more to the list of universal fairy-tales!

2

In many ways it wasn't a disagreeable life she and Bernard led in the snow-castle. The *table d'hôte*, if monotonous, was of first-class quality, and days of mouse-nibblings left the south side of the cheese barely indented. Through the long nights, upon sofa or in sleeping-bag, they slept perfectly – of course each in a fur coat; and indeed it would have interested any zoologist to see how quickly these Nature's gifts responded to the Antarctic climate by thickening and fluffing out; soon Miss Bianca was looking quite like a powder-puff, and Bernard like a door-mat. But however physically comfortable, still the dreadful, haunting thought, at least in Miss Bianca's mind, persisted : *no one knew where they were!*

Was anyone even *wondering* where they were?

3

Certainly the Boy was, at any rate about Miss Bianca. Far off in an Embassy bedroom the Boy so tossed and turned, his mother the Ambassadress came from the middle of a State Banquet, to sit by his pillow and try to soothe him.

'Lie still and go to sleep, my darling!' said she.

'Miss Bianca will come back, as she always does . . .'

'Only I don't know where she's *gone*,' persisted the Boy. 'I do think she might have left a note!'

'Perhaps she did,' said the Ambassadress. 'But her notes are so very small, if she left one on your pillow, for instance, any of your big yawns might have puffed it away, if not swallowed it up!'

'If it's inside me,' suggested the Boy eagerly, 'couldn't I be X-rayed?'

'Certainly,' said his mother – who rather wanted him to be X-rayed in any case; he'd come back from playing hockey with a bruise on his side and she feared a broken rib, even though the Ambassador said Nonsense. 'You shall be X-rayed tomorrow morning,' she promised, 'and then we may know all about it!'

But all the X-ray doctor reported was just a hair-line crack not worth worrying about, though no more hockey for a week or two.

'Didn't you find a note inside me?' demanded the Boy.

'A note?' repeated the doctor, surprised.

'In very small writing,' said the Boy, 'signed Miss Bianca – or perhaps just M.B., as she does her poems.'

'A trifle feverish nonetheless,' decided the doctor. 'Keep him a day in bed . . .'

'But how can I possibly,' protested the Boy agitatedly, 'stay in bed, when I ought to be making enquiries after her high and low?'

'*Several* days,' said the doctor.

The Ambassadress was as a rule a wonderful

mother. For instance, she'd always appreciated Miss Bianca and never been jealous of her; was even beginning to be troubled herself about Miss Bianca. But when a doctor says several days in bed, it is the doctor mothers listen to rather than to their offspring however agitated. (Indeed the more the more, so to speak.) Immediately upon their return to the Embassy the Boy was put firmly to bed and out of action.

If he'd been in normal action, he'd certainly have questioned his friend the chauffeur, who it may be remembered had actually sighted Miss Bianca in the laurel-wreath, and who could thus have offered a first clue to her distressing whereabouts. But confined to bed as he was, the Boy could enquire only of a footman and a housemaid – both too stupid even to have noticed the Porcelain Pagoda unoccupied.

Certainly Bernard's flat in the cigar-cabinet was noticed as being unoccupied : the accumulating milk bottles outside his front door – (no note left for the milkman) – quite soon attracted neighbourly attention, and if they'd gone *on* accumulating might have aroused alarm as well. However, a Judge's wife living in the drawer above thought they made the stairs look so untidy, she took it upon herself to phone the Dairy to stop delivering until further orders.

('You did, my dear?' said the Judge uneasily, when she reported this, and also looking uneasily at the four half-pints she'd brought up in her shopping-basket, for it struck him as very near Petty Theft. 'Wasn't that a trifle officious?' 'Not at all, my love!'

said his wife briskly. 'If he's put to the trouble of re-ordering, it may teach him not to be so untidy!')

The stairs tidy as usual, all Bernard's other neighbours (with whom the Judge's wife didn't mix) assumed him to be at home and taking in his milk as usual.

The absence of both its ex-Secretary and ex-Madam Chairwoman from the next MPAS General Meeting was equally *noticed*, but equally without creating alarm. The incoming Madam Chairwoman in fact thought it just like Miss Bianca's delicacy not to draw attention from the platform by appearing in the body of the hall; so did the incoming Secretary appreciate Bernard's absence, though putting it down not so much to tact as the fascinations of a new stamp-album. The regular Item First on the Agenda, Cheering of Prisoners — let alone rescuing of! — was simply passed over; for once, the Society had no knowledge of any prisoners anywhere, let alone in the Antarctic!

As for Nils, who of course knew more than anyone, he didn't wonder or worry at all, having read in the papers of the Poet's safe return to Oslo. The Poet safe back, Nils naturally presumed Miss Bianca and Bernard safe back too, the one in her Porcelain Pagoda, the other in his cigar-cabinet flat. Nils often *thought* about his old friends, but only by way of thinking how clever and brave (and evidently successful) they'd been; whilst the Poet himself, not having even recognized his saviours, didn't think of them at all.

There remained the helicopter captain, who with-

out actually *looking* for Miss Bianca and Bernard
might yet have rescued them so to speak on the side.
Weekly the big whirly-bird still clattered overhead;
and as Humbert patted up more and more battlements and buttresses to his snow-castle, the whole
complex, centring round the red Dutch cheese, seen
from above must have looked like a huge white
daisy, and such an unusual specimen of Antarctic
flora as any botanist on board would have insisted
on being let down to investigate, and Bernard and
Miss Bianca could have hitched a lift. But unfor-
tunately the helicopters just carried the usual hydrographer and photographer and fisheries-expert.

 In short, it was up to Bernard and Miss Bianca to

rescue themselves . . . Only as Bernard had wondered as early as Camp One, *how?*

How they escaped at least from the snow-castle will be described in the next chapter.

CHAPTER 8

New Friends

The day had started ill enough with Bernard knocking himself out. Though the castle walls were by now higher than ever, and his and Miss Bianca's poor success at escalading them has been described, Bernard never knew when he was beat. As soon as Humbert padded home to lunch –

'*This* time I'm going to start with a running jump!' declared Bernard doggedly.

He positioned himself as far back as possible, warmed up with a few skips like a bowler before starting the run-up, leapt half his own height and positively hurled himself though the air, no longer bowler but ball! The impetus carried him at least a centimetre beyond his hitherto highest mark, and at least three beyond Miss Bianca's; for an instant he teetered there, hanging on with tooth and claw – but then down again slithered – or rather (the impetus acting in reverse), crashed . . .

'My dear Bernard, are you seriously injured?' cried Miss Bianca, hastening to his side and feeling his pulse.

The solicitude in her voice, also that delicate pressure on his wrist, revived him almost immediately. Gazing up into her great dark eyes so anxiously bent upon him, Bernard only wished himself back in Camp One to look up some phrase of the Immortal Bard's with which to express his emotions, probably out of *Romeo and Juliet*. As things were, however, he but suggested, as soon as he was on his legs again, taking her round the cheese.

Miss Bianca hadn't been all round the cheese for some time. She had exercise enough, and as a promenade it struck her as too much like going round a supermarket. She was quite content to shop, so to speak, at its southern branch, or side. What she would now have seen on the north side was in fact a heart with an arrow through it, flanked by two B's, a labour of love Bernard had laboured nibbling at whenever Miss Bianca was asleep or not looking. He hadn't yet showed it her because the time never seemed quite right; once just as he was going to Humbert turned up, and another time she began talking about the Boy. But now seemed the very moment.

'Just round the cheese, there's something I'd like to show you, Miss Bianca,' said Bernard huskily.

'If you've swallowed anything more than *snow*, pray don't hesitate to get rid of it,' said Miss Bianca kindly. 'I won't look!'

'I haven't,' said Bernard, 'and it's only a step . . .'

Under this renewed urging Miss Bianca of course consented, though with so obviously slight enthusiasm, even as she took his arm Bernard's own inside heart misgave him. Would she really be pleased, or touched, by what he himself now saw might appear as but a piece of juvenilia? Hearing her heave an involuntary sigh, Bernard disappointedly recognized that a day so ill begun probably wasn't one for giving Valentines on.

'Or perhaps not just now,' said he, 'when we're both a bit exhausted. That is, *I*'m all right, but I'm afraid I frightened you, Miss Bianca, and perhaps you'd rather just sit down?'

Miss Bianca not only did so (a little snow *bergère*, or armchair, at once forming beneath her), but sighed again more deeply still. However, the last thing she wanted was to cause Bernard unnecessary remorse.

'You alarmed me indeed!' said she, attempting a smile. 'But if I *do* appear a little low, I assure you 'tis not due to any sudden shock, but rather to a cumulation of mental distress. The sense of isolation, the enormous distance from home,' confessed Miss Bianca, 'are beginning to tell on my nerves.'

'I worry too,' said Bernard understandingly. 'For instance, *I* ought to be sub-letting my flat, only how, as you say at such a distance, can I get hold of a reliable estate agent?'

'Moreover,' confessed Miss Bianca, 'though I admit I'd come to regard the MPAS as rather a bore, to be entirely cut off from any organized group whatever does make one feel a little *lonely* . . . My dear Bernard, could we not incorporate ourselves into an Overseas Branch?'

Bernard was so glad to see her looking a little encouraged by the notion, he'd have willingly incorporated himself into a Pop Group, and so then and there they did.

Miss Bianca was of course Madam Chairwoman,

and Bernard offered to be Secretary, Treasurer, Caterer, Director of Publications, and anything else he could think of, drawing the line only at President of the Ladies' Guild. He next assisted Miss Bianca to her feet, announced a Special Meeting, took the Minutes as read, cleared his throat to announce Item on the Agenda No. 1, and paused.

In the admittedly Special circumstances, he couldn't think of any items whatever! To make matters worse, he could feel Miss Bianca, at his side, beginning to tremble all over, he hoped only with nerves, but what if with *tears*? He couldn't even offer her his handkerchief, she had it on already. A faint squeak confirmed his worst apprehensions; he forced himself to look round, and to his immense relief saw Madam Chairwoman shaking not with tears, but with suppressed laughter!

'I didn't know I sounded as funny as all that,' said Bernard, rather stiffly all the same. 'I was only trying to do my best . . .'

'Dear Mr Secretary, pray forgive me,' apologized Miss Bianca. ' 'Twas not at you I laughed, but at myself! For what could be greater folly, or more ludicrous, than to preside over a Meeting with absolutely nothing on the Agenda, and not a single auditor present!'

At which precise moment a certain shuffling, shifting-of-feet sound impinged upon her and Bernard's ears; and looking up, both observed at least a score of Adélie penguins attentively ranged on the bluff beyond the moat . . .

The little Adélie penguins are the most inquisitive creatures alive. Any unusual sight attracts them as pollen does bees. The snow-castle in the first place an object of interest, how much *more* interesting to find it inhabited! Thus they were every bit as attentive and expectant as any similar number of mice ranged on match-box benches in the Moot-house. Their *appearance* was actually far smarter. In their black-and-white plumage – as if in black tail-coats and stiff white shirts – they looked to Miss Bianca like a whole corps of Ambassadors!

She instinctively bowed. All the penguins bowed back.

She cleared her throat to address them. All the penguins turned round and marched away!

'Dear me!' said Miss Bianca. 'I don't think much of their manners!'

'Nor me neither,' growled Bernard.

'And when the tallest (evidently their *doyen*, or leader),' mused Miss Bianca, 'quite reminded me of our own Ambassador! But *autres pays, autres moeurs*,' she added, which being translated from the French means that foreign parts are by their nature foreign, and so not to be judged by home standards. In Oriental regions, for example, it is as ill-mannered to go to church without taking one's shoes off as in others (Occidental) without taking off one's hat. Miss Bianca was a thorough woman of the world, and indeed was glad she'd said nothing harsher, when within minutes not only the original twenty but about the same number more came marching back. With such a wonderful sight to be seen, they'd just gone to fetch a few friends before anything really interesting occurred.

'Good evening,' now began the Leader courteously. 'May we join in whatever's going on?'

'Why, certainly,' said Miss Bianca, rapidly collecting her wits. 'Since this happens to be an *Open* meeting of the MPAS.'

'Our Moulting Penguins' Assistance Scheme? How very good of you to take an interest in it!' said the Leader appreciatively.

'No, no!' said Miss Bianca, and eager to nip any misunderstanding in the bud, at once in a few well-chosen words described the aims, organization and achievements of the Mouse Prisoners' Aid Society. That is, her words were certainly well chosen, but not exactly few; it was actually one of the longest speeches Miss Bianca ever made, as she found herself

78

drawn into descriptions of all the various rescues the Society had in its time pulled off. The Adélies listened as enthralled as Humbert to a fairy-tale; and being besides outstandingly inquisitive, outstandingly sociable, as soon as she ended were clamouring to join this other MPAS too.

However flattered by this brilliant result of her eloquence, Miss Bianca hesitated.

('Why ever not?' muttered Bernard, aside. 'Forty new members at one fell swoop! I'll enroll 'em at once.'

'Forty indeed!' murmured Miss Bianca. 'Just think of all the paper-work involved!'

'Don't bother about that,' said practical Bernard, 'there *isn't* any paper. I'll enroll 'em verbally, all in one bunch . . .')

So now it was Bernard's turn to make a speech, or rather to issue a few concise instructions, which he did without further delay.

'All those wishing to become members of the Mouse Prisoners' Aid Society, raise the right flipper,' directed Bernard.

Every penguin did so. Some in their enthusiasm raised both.

'Proposed by the Secretary, seconded by the Treasurer, carried unanimously, and Bob's your uncle,' said Bernard briskly.

Miss Bianca couldn't help feeling this rather unceremonious, but the penguins' Leader nodded approvingly.

'Most expeditious and clear,' said he. 'Now we

shall all listen with even keener interest, as you describe what particular prisoners need rescuing hereabouts.'

Bernard looked at Miss Bianca. Miss Bianca looked at Bernard. At the same moment, with dismaying force, it dawned on both what the missing Item No. 1 on the MPAS Agenda should have been: Rescue of its Secretary and Madam Chairwoman!

3

'I suppose we'll have to tell 'em it's us?' muttered Bernard.

'Yet how embarrassing!' murmured Miss Bianca. 'Also may it not appear as if our whole motive in interesting them was purely self-centred?'

'I must say it's a bit of a pity the Poet's got away already,' acknowledged Bernard. 'All the same, I don't believe they're birds to split pin-feathers . . .'

Above, across the moat, all the new MPAS members stood eagerly waiting for an answer. Seeing Miss Bianca for the moment too confused to speak, Bernard took the bull by the horns, or cat by the tail.

'The *original* prisoner,' he explained, 'and thanks to Madam Chairwoman's heroic endeavours, has been rescued already. Now it's just us who're still imprisoned. In fact, the long and the short of it is, we can't get out of here.'

Fortunately he was quite right in thinking the little Adélies woudln't much mind *whom* they rescued, so long as they rescued someone!

'Why, no more you can!' chattered all the little Adélies. 'Look, they can't get out!' they told each other. 'But we'll soon see to *that*,' they cried encouragingly, 'just mind and stand clear!'

With which words one after the other began tobogganing down into the moat, then skiing up the castle battlements, until the latter were quite breached, and crumbling outwards into the moat formed such a causeway as any mouse could cross with ease.

Easily Bernard and Miss Bianca did so. The bluff beyond, after being so toboggan-downed, presented no more difficulty; within moments they gained its lip; and Miss Bianca had even breath enough left for a short but heart-felt expression of gratitude.

'Dear friends, or as I may now call you, Fellow Members,' cried she, 'your swift and resourceful co-operation will ever be remembered in the annals of our Society, where Bernard shall write all about it as soon as we get home. Meanwhile our thanks, and ever thanks, and still more thanks again!'

'Only where do we go from here?' muttered Bernard.

He didn't really mean to be heard, even by Miss Bianca, but he muttered louder than he knew, and the whole front row of penguins unhesitatingly answered.

'Why, to the Ball, of course!'

4

Adélie penguins lead very full social lives. Their engagement-books, if they'd had engagement-books, would have been as stuffed as the Ambassador's. The excitement of enrolling in one more Society just pepped them up for the entertainment already laid on : and without waiting for formal acceptance of their kind invitation, they at once carried Bernard and Miss Bianca along with them to their Palais de Danse in an icicle-chandeliered grot.

CHAPTER 9

The Penguin Ball

'What a Ball, what a Ball, what a happening!' chattered the Adélies, dozens and dozens all skidding and bobbing over the beautifully polished floor. It was smooth as a skating-rink, a thin layer of ice that under the shelter of an overhanging ledge never thawed out or grew lumpy. The icicle-chandeliers were more brilliantly spectacular than any Miss Bianca'd ever seen in an Embassy, and the dancers certainly far *rowdier*! 'Whoopee!' shouted the happy, rowdy penguins. 'Whoops outside for a conga and whoops back in again for another square dance!'

The caller for the square dance was a middle-aged, rather thick-set penguin named Am (short for Amundsen), who was so good at it, and so much in demand, he could have been out every night in the week only his wife objected. Music was supplied by a traditionally blind old penguin fiddling on a mussel-shell strung with mermaids' hair-combings; there was also a Ladies' Three-Piece Orchestra which equipped with similar instruments played for waltzes.

'First choose your partner, stand in a row,'
  (called Am)
'Flippers across and off you go!
  Weed-foot, web-foot, the fun's begun,
  So get yourselves ready for Figure One!'
Figure One was Icicles.
  'See you stand up cold and straight,
  Don't touch your partner, don't touch
    your mate!
  Chassez back-to-back till sudden comes
    the thaw
  And don't you feel much warmer than you
    ever did before?'

Since at the words 'comes the thaw', all the penguins turned and hugged each other as closely as their chubbiness allowed, they certainly did!

Figure Two was Pebbles.

> *'Now lay a pebble at your lady's feet,*
> *Ain't she purty, ain't she neat?*
> *Pebble after pebble right up to a score,*
> *Twenty-ONE and she's yours for evermore!'*

— after which, and about a dozen other figures, Am promenaded them home to such universal enjoyment, he had to begin all over again . . .

Despite every disparity in size, who but Miss Bianca was the belle of the Ball! Her elegant tripping round a partner's feet — her statuesque rigidity standing up cold and straight — aroused universal admiration.

'Only do take that great shawl off!' begged the penguins. 'We can't *see* you properly, in that great shawl!'

Miss Bianca had grown so warm, she was quite glad to untie Bernard's handkerchief and put it in the cloakroom, especially as the next dance announced was a waltz. She couldn't help knowing she waltzed quite beautifully! Also her partner this time was to be the Leader himself, so naturally all eyes would be upon her even more than ever.

It was a lovely waltz, rather like 'The Blue Danube'.

> *'O snowflakes so white, so white, so white!'*

began to sing all the circling penguins,

> *'O stars up above so bright, so bright, so bright!*

High in the sky, who knows why,
But O my what a beautiful sight!'

Before the reprise, however, the Leader suggested taking Miss Bianca outside for a breath of air.

'One isn't as young as one was!' he sighed apologetically.

'Which of us is?' agreed Miss Bianca. She was beginning to feel exhausted herself (no wonder, after such a day!) and now no longer buoyed up by music and admiration even cast an appreciative thought towards that once-odious rocking-chair. A few flakes of snow began to fall.

'To tell you the truth, m'dear,' added the Leader humorously, 'I brought you out here with every intention of *flirting* with you! Only now it seems I'm not up to it!'

'Such a confidence pleases me far better,' said Miss Bianca quite truthfully, for if there is anything more exhausting than waltzing when one is tired it is flirting when one is tired; and she tactfully added, to give him an excuse for not even having to make conversation, that without his calming-down presence the Ball seemed to be getting rowdier than ever.

'So it is,' agreed the Leader, cocking an ear towards renewed shouts of Whoopee. 'And we certainly don't want complaints from our distinguished visitors the polar bears! In fact, now that your escort has joined us, I believe I'd better return.'

As he bowed and went in again Miss Bianca perceived Bernard indeed at her side. (Bernard's own part in the Ball had been too undistinguished to rate description. The only dance he knew how to was the polka, and it hadn't yet come up. A young-lady penguin trying to teach him the square dance gave up even before Pebbles.) Owing to Miss Bianca's on-the-other-hand brilliant success he'd hardly been able to exchange a word with her, and so was more than ever glad to have her to himself for a bit, especially when she almost at once raised a point which had been bothering him all along, otherwise he might have learnt at least Icicles.

'What a charming Ball!' said Miss Bianca. 'What true gaiety and high spirits! Yet I confess I should enjoy myself more if we weren't still so far from home.'

'My thought exactly,' said Bernard. 'They're very good chaps, these penguins, but one can't feel membership of the MPAS really meaningful to them, that is, not in the way of *sticking* to rescue-work. Whoopee and that's that with 'em.'

'In many ways I agree,' agreed Miss Bianca. 'Yet be fair, Bernard; remember that in *their* view they've finished rescuing us already, as so they have, at least from the snow-castle! If caught up in their own social whirl they do indeed check out, I for one shall never bear them any grudge!'

'Nor me neither,' said Bernard. 'Only as you said yourself, Miss Bianca, or as I thought you were going to say, where do we go from here?'

For a moment both thought in silence. It was quieter too, behind them in the ballroom, where the Leader's return had evidently calming-downly operated.

'Actually with the weather looking like it is,'

suggested Bernard, peering up through the now quite thick-and-fast falling snow, 'why not *back* to the castle, for at least temporary shelter while we work out our next move? It wasn't altogether bashed down.'

It must be admitted that he was thinking partly of the Dutch cheese. He'd always felt it a friend. But Miss Bianca (whose affinity was rather with Shakespeare) shuddered.

'Back to that *prison*? Never!' cried she. 'To Camp One, yes, perhaps . . . In which direction would you say it lies?'

Both strained their eyes, peering through snowflakes now ever thicker-and-faster falling, also beginning to whirl about before the rising wind.

'Dashed if I know,' confessed Bernard.

'In any case it can't be much farther off than the castle,' argued Miss Bianca. 'We must still be within a short march!'

So in fact they were; but by now Camp One was buried under such a blanket of snow as even the burning words of *Antony and Cleopatra* insufficed to thaw.

'In any case we can hardly see before our noses,' said Bernard. 'Speaking of which, I do believe I might be able to smell that cheese quite yards and yards off. You know I never like to make you do anything you don't want, Miss Bianca, but I'm sure it's our best bet.'

'And are probably right,' acknowledged Miss Bianca. 'Still, let me make just a cast towards Camp One!'

So saying, she tripped hardily forth, only a few paces, but naturally turning her back; and in those few split seconds, without his handkerchief round her shoulders, became totally invisible! 'Stop, stop, Miss Bianca!' yelled Bernard, but his voice was carried away by the wind, and Miss Bianca ran on. So now did Bernard begin to run, he intended after her, but the snow blotted out her tiny footprints as fast as she imprinted them, and amid the whirling flakes he lost all bearings. As Miss Bianca bravely hurried on, so did Bernard, only in *the opposite direction*!

Through what was now practically a blizzard, and Miss Bianca without so much as a shawl to protect her!

2

'Ma, what's happening to my Fairies?' mewed Humbert, tucked safely under his mother's furry tum. Above the pair of them crouched the big father bear, presenting to the weather such a thick rug of insulating fur, down where Humbert was it felt quite cosy. But he was a loyal, affectionate little cub.

'Keep quiet, my love, don't wriggle so,' said his mother. 'Hasn't your Dad always told us to lie quite still, under a blizzard?'

'But I ought to be out looking for them,' persisted Humbert, just like the Boy in other circumstances. 'Didn't *you* tell me, if I kept pets I must be responsible? Now that it's so dreadful outside, whatever

can have happened to them?'

'Why, they'll have been turned into snowflakes,'
said his mother resourcefully. 'Isn't that what always
happens to Fairies?'

It seemed reasonable enough to Humbert. He put
down his blackberry nose again and snored.

3

If only Bernard and Miss Bianca had at least been *together*, to aid and encourage one another! But every painfully gained inch but took them farther apart, until each collapsed from cold and fatigue quite, quite alone . . .

What could save either from an icy death?

CHAPTER 10

At Death's Door!

What saved Bernard was the door-mat thickness of his new Antarctic coat. He had actually almost reached the snow-castle when not his nose but his legs so definitely packed up, even a new quite strong whiff of Dutch cheese was powerless to reactivate them and he utterly collapsed. But as usual when

Bernard collapsed his weight scooped out a little natural sleeping-bag, in which, under the snow settling like a canopy, his new Antarctic coat insulated him as in temporary cold storage.

Miss Bianca, however, was far lighter, and for all her powder-puff appearance far less furrily protected. Hitherto, her shawl had made up the difference, but where was that useful object now? In the cloakroom at the Palais de Danse.

She was also far tireder than Bernard, having danced so many more dances after an equally punishing day. (Usually before a Ball Miss Bianca spent the afternoon lying down.) Moreover *her* slender limbs gave way upon a patch of snow so hard and unyielding as to be indistinguishable from ice, and try as she might, employing all her failing strength, she couldn't scoop up even a slight blizzard-break ....

She still didn't mean to be found frozen stiff as a board like Nils's deplorable cousin in the refrigerator. With a last effort Miss Bianca drew up her tail in a graceful curve, ere devoting her last sentient moments to composing a last poem.

POEM COMPOSED BY MISS BIANCA
WHILST EXPECTING TO FREEZE TO DEATH

How icy steals th'Antarctic chill
From limb to limb, in every part!
Not long, now, ere Death's fatal touch
Strikes Miss Bianca to the heart!

M. B.

Then she felt quite ashamed at closing a not unsuccessful literary career on such a weak, self-pitying note. Even if none ever read or heard her last opus, she owed it to her Muse to end more gallantly! So she began again.

If die I must (as who must not,
    Both king and churl, both large and less?)
    Then like a rodent let me go,
    Undaunted still 'mid ice and snow,
Glad to have shared the rodent lot,
    And known a rodent's happiness!

M. B.

'*Much* better!' thought Miss Bianca. 'And dear me, I believe I've invented a new verse-form! What a pity I shan't have time to explore it further!'

For as the Antarctic chill went on stealing, she felt death indeed nigh – nigher even than when she'd faced drowning in rose-water or being squashed by a railway-guard's boot. After how many hair's-breadth escapes, in how many desperate adventures, death was upon her at last!

However, the glow of achievement at inventing a new verse-form so warmed her, she stayed alive a few moments more, just long enough, in fact, to feel the surface-crust of snow crack under a heavy tread, and to sense, rather than see, looming above her, a huge protective presence.

She sensed no more; was not even aware, as a great black foot lifted and stamped, of being borne down as in a descending elevator to regions where neither snow nor wind, nor indeed any natural sort of weather, ever penetrated . . .

CHAPTER II

A Very Important Person

Miss Bianca in fact woke completely thawed out in
the cosiest also most elegant bed imaginable! – a
large oyster-shell layered first with dried moss (to
give spring, like a spring-mattress), then with eider-
duck down (for warmth without weight). Before she
opened her eyes there was a moment when she
almost fancied herself back between the silk sheets
of her own Porcelain Pagoda; but of course she
wasn't, as a first wide-awake glance at once told her.
Not porcelain but crystalline walls surrounded her
couch, forming a little alcove within a larger crystalline chamber, also there were no other articles of
furniture such as a lady is accustomed to, not even
a mirror, though this didn't matter much, since each
shimmering wall-surface reflected as well as the best
pier-glass. 'Evidently I'm staying with someone of
high importance!' thought Miss Bianca. 'Whose
hospitality I fear I must have accepted all too
cavalierly! But where,' she mentally added, as the
events of the previous night grew clearer, 'where, O
where, is Bernard?'

The reader knows. In cold storage. But what
occurred to Miss Bianca was that perchance he too
had been taken in by the same generous, unknown
host, whom she became more than ever eager to
meet and thank. So she at once got up (even though

it was quite hard to quit that downy couch), and made the best toilet she could before seeking their benefactor out. Though she hadn't her overnight bag, a stray pin-feather amongst the eiderdown sufficed for brush, and with her coat at least in proper order, she ventured eagerly forth.

If the chamber of which the alcove formed part had seemed large enough, it was as nothing to the size of the chamber adjoining. Here the ceiling was so high Miss Bianca couldn't even see it – as indeed it needed to be, to accommodate the enormous three-foot-six height of the person, or presence, there obviously awaiting her . . .

'Twas an Emperor Penguin!

Miss Bianca, who together with the Boy took in the *National Geographic Magazine*, recognized him at once: not only by his stature, but by the flash of orange (like some distinguished Order, such as the Golden Fleece) at his throat. She instinctively curtseyed. Miss Bianca curtseyed so gracefully, it was quite a pity that even with her high diplomatic connections she rarely met a reigning monarch, while for anyone of lower rank rightly felt a bow quite sufficient. Now, as the Emperor bowed back, she felt *that* quite sufficient too.

'I trust you slept well?' enquired the Emperor courteously.

'Indeed I did!' replied Miss Bianca. 'Untroubled,' she added, 'even by the thought that I must have appeared less than polite at our first meeting, which actually,' she confessed, 'I scarcely recall! Being, as you no doubt observed, frozen practically stiff.'

'If I may say so, in a remarkably graceful attitude,' said the Emperor. 'But what a night for ex-Madam President Miss Bianca to be out in!'

'You know me, then?' cried Miss Bianca, quite astounded. 'How is it possible?'

'I happen to have a rather good Intelligence Service,' said the Emperor casually. 'What the tides don't tell me the whirlwinds will, and really those Adélies are the greatest gossips alive. I must say I felt a little surprised at such a personage as yourself consorting with them at all.'

'They were still very good friends to me,' said Miss Bianca, 'though I admit slightly scatterbrained! May I ask whether your truly-life-saving hospitality has included the ex-*Secretary* of the MPAS? I refer of course to Bernard, whom, if you know of *me*, you must doubtless know of too?'

But the Emperor evidently didn't; nor, to Miss Bianca's distress, showed the least sign of wanting to. He showed no interest whatever in Bernard, but merely rather brushing-offly remarked that he never entertained more than one guest at a time, owing to the narrowness of his quarters.

'Which you might still care to see over,' suggested the Emperor, 'that is, if sufficiently refreshed?'

Of course Miss Bianca replied that nothing would please her more. Though her anxiety about Bernard was now increasing every moment, she recognized her obligations as a guest; and moreover suspected the Emperor of such an understatement as when the owner of a Rolls-Royce refers to his little buggy, so that she felt quite curious as well. Miss Bianca

suspected the Emperor's quarters to be quite palatial, and was at once proved right as he led her on into a further and even huger apartment.

'What I call my Gallery of Fame,' explained the Emperor. 'In each of these niches round the walls the bust of *another* Emperor! Trajan, you see, and Marcus Aurelius – both Roman of course – '

'Succeeded the one by Hadrian, the other by Commodus,' supplied Miss Bianca. The Boy's Ancient History period was from 10 to 11 every Tuesday.

'What a pleasure to meet a kindred spirit!' said the Emperor. 'I knew you'd be interested. But let me help you to examine them more nearly. If you permit – ?'

So speaking, he bent and scooped Miss Bianca up on one big, black, leathery flipper. Though he hadn't *waited* for permission it was in the circumstances a perfectly reasonable act, since from floor level she could see practically nothing of the busts at all, while the moving platform (so to speak) was so firm and broad, Miss Bianca felt physically perfectly safe. Yet for some reason, for the first time, she felt a vague alarm. Really she'd been picked up just as casually as a chess-player picks up a pawn! However, she was truly interested to examine, while thus borne from niche to niche, the succession of Roman noses therein enshrined.

These were in fact the only features recognizable: the rest of each head was simply a chunk of granite of roughly the right size and shape. In fact the more closely she looked, Miss Bianca decided that any chunk of granite with a high-bridged bump on it was a Roman bust to the Emperor Penguin! 'How is it possible he can so delude himself?' thought she. ' 'Tis little short of madness!' But of course she kept these awkward thoughts to herself, and just looked as admiring as possible.

'And here,' pursued the Emperor, halting before a rather less bumpy bust, 'is perhaps my greatest treasure of all : Theodore the Second. No doubt you've heard of the Byzantine Empire also?'

'Flourished A D 630 to 1204,' supplied Miss Bianca.

'And then declined,' said the Emperor sadly. 'Times change,' he ruminated, 'empires come and go – consider too the Babylonian and the Egyptian! Only mine shall endure to all eternity! So you see what a terrible burden I bear,' he added, 'the whole Antarctic on my shoulders! Uneasy indeed lies the head that wears a crown!'

'Now I see you share *my* passion,' exclaimed Miss Bianca, quite encouraged, and hoping to give the conversation a more rational turn, 'since you quote Shakespeare!'

'Shakespeare? Never heard of him,' said the Emperor. 'It must be he who's quoting *me*. I've said that more times than I can remember.'

Miss Bianca, who knew how many phrases first minted by poets have seeped into popular currency, couldn't resist asking whether he also sometimes said 'How sweet is the Shepherd's sweet lot' (William Blake).

'Certainly I do; but you mean an *oyster's* lot,'

corrected the Emperor. 'There indeed, in an oyster-bed, what perfect peace, what calm, what tranquillity! The least irritation, a mere grain of sand, effortlessly transformed into a pearl – the steadiest currency the Deep has ever known! I've often thought,' he added ruminatively, 'of indenturing a labour-corps of cuttle-fish, and sending 'em up to the Red Sea, to slip between the shells as they open to the tide and fetch the pearls back to *me*. Of course they might get a tentacle nipped off now and then, but it would certainly be a useful source of revenue; quite worth a few cuttle-fish without tentacles at all! When they'd have to find a new name for themselves, such as cripple-fish!'

As Miss Bianca felt the ground (or rather flipper) beneath her feet quiver with mirth –

'Would you mind if I get down?' she asked. 'I have never had a head for heights . . .'

'Of course!' said the Emperor courteously, at once lowering her to the ground. 'Unless,' he added, scooping her up again, 'you'd care to complete the tour first?'

How could Miss Bianca refuse? Obviously she couldn't, now suddenly lofted back on that broad, black, leathery flipper! As a rule Miss Bianca thoroughly appreciated leatheriness (as she appreciated all natural substances, such as amber, and bamboo, and wood-shavings), in preference to plastics; but there was something about the Emperor's flipper's leatheriness that sent a shudder up her tail. She found it worse than wearisome, being forced to complete the tour, and was relieved to find the last niche empty.

'Reserved for yourself, no doubt?' said Miss Bianca.

She made the suggestion only to be polite; and was therefore all the more astonished when the Emperor turned on her a look of absolute fury!

'A mere *bust*?' cried the Emperor wrathfully. 'A mere *bust*, and *underground*? *My* statue shall rear high above the whole Antarctic!'

'I've no doubt it will,' said Miss Bianca soothingly.

'Only where do I find the labour?' demanded the Emperor, not soothed at all. 'Have I been able to indenture even those cuttle-fish yet? Forgive me,' he added, with an obvious effort at self-control, 'for intruding my cares on you; your extreme sympathy led me on. Shall we go round just once more?'

Miss Bianca felt she really couldn't.

'Enthralling as the experience has been,' said she, 'perhaps not just at the moment . . . Also welcome as your hospitality has been, I fear to impose upon it! Especially since my colleague the ex-Secretary of the MPAS is doubtless even now searching for me up above.'

'In such a blizzard as this, up above no mouse would stand a dog's chance,' said the Emperor callously. 'If you insist I'll have his corpse looked for; but meanwhile *you* shall remain my house-guest as long as I like!'

Not as long as *she* liked, noted Miss Bianca; as long as the Emperor liked! But at the moment (no bolder alternative offering, and to gain time), she exercised a feminine privilege and said she had a headache and must really lie down.

'Precisely what I was about to advise,' said the Emperor Penguin, just as though he hadn't an instant before invited her to make a third tour of his horrid Gallery of Fame. 'Lie down and refresh yourself indeed, after your trying experience among those common little Adélies! There is ample time before us for further enjoyable conversation!'

Miss Bianca almost smiled. To *her*, the trying experience had been almost freezing to death, and she felt her present predicament almost as bad! Little did the Emperor guess her thoughts, as she once again gracefully curtseyed, before withdrawing to her oyster-shell couch!

She customarily took a nap in the afternoon after a Ball (as well as one before; which was why she always appeared so fresh and elegant), and as a rule had no difficulty in dropping at once into a light refreshing slumber amid the thistledown cushions of her chaise-longue. But now, though eiderdown was just as soft, she couldn't sleep a wink for worrying about where Bernard was . . .

Had Bernard been conscious, he of course would have been reciprocally worrying about Miss Bianca. Only he was comatose, that is absolutely *un*-conscious, in cold storage, in a stupor from which only an earthquake could have roused him ere he finally expired stiff as a board like Nils's cousin. For the first time in all their joint adventurings, Bernard was no more help to Miss Bianca than a broken match. Temporarily separated from her by a Ranee's selfishness,* he'd tramped seven hours every day just to keep in heartening touch; even when she was carried off by the Diamond Duchess, he'd at least been able to take action by going after her disguised as a knife-grinder.† In cold storage he could do nothing whatever.

And was not Miss Bianca equally, though more comfortably, powerless?

'Alas!' sighed she into the eiderdown. ''Tis this separation that is worst to bear of all! Yet whom to blame but myself?' sighed Miss Bianca, and uncontrollably composed a brief remorseful verse.

BRIEF VERSE COMPOSED BY MISS BIANCA
WHILST WORRIED ABOUT BERNARD

Bernard, where art thou? Wandering alone
Mid'st th'icy blast that chills the heart to stone?
All, all alone? Alas to me what grief
That ere I cast aside thy spotted handkerchief!

M. B.

Well might Miss Bianca regret her impulsive but still at the time quite natural action, but was she herself paying any less dearly for it?

* See *Miss Bianca in the Orient.*
† See *Miss Bianca.*

Whilst I myself,' (added Miss Bianca)
                    'house-guest of majesty,
Am no less wretched, powerless, than thee!

'Twas indeed about the worst dire peril even Bernard and Miss Bianca had ever found themselves in . . .

CHAPTER 12

Death Defied!

Bernard was at least unconscious; Miss Bianca's awareness of their desperate plight had so to speak to do double duty, whilst her nerves increasingly frayed. The Emperor Penguin seemed quite to dote upon her – which Miss Bianca would normally have found gratifying, since she'd always cultivated the social tact that made her acceptable company to both high and low – and what company could be higher than that of an Emperor, however mad? (Dementia wasn't even unusual amongst crowned heads, thought Miss Bianca, recalling Caligula who made his horse a consul, and King Ludwig of Bavaria who imagined himself Siegfried, and poor King George of England who sometimes imagined himself a teapot.) But there was small gratification in being doted upon merely as a captive audience, as Miss Bianca, touring the Gallery of Fame for the eleventh or twelfth time, now suspected to be the case! She grew as much affronted and bored as anxious and distressed.

Also she was steadily losing weight.

It was one of the features of life underground that there seemed to be no meals. Had Miss Bianca known more of penguin ways, this would have surprised her less; penguins can go as much as twenty-eight days without any nourishment at all. Of course she would still have been just as hungry; and now might have absolutely famished, but for her interior-spring mattress.

Painful as it is to relate, the famous, fastidious Miss Bianca was reduced to eating *moss*.

Not even fresh moss; dried moss.

The taste was slightly medicinal, like penicillin.

Miss Bianca shuddered whenever she took a nibble, but fortunately, and like so many other unpalatable foods, it was quite highly nourishing, and even the small amount she forced herself to swallow sufficed to keep her strength if not her weight up. To drink, she had but the occasional drop of condensation forming on the crystalline walls.

'When people speak of palatial *luxury*,' thought Miss Bianca, 'how little do they know!'

Bitterer even than the taste of moss, however – more chilling even than the temperature of her drinking water – was the fact that never for a moment could she interest the Emperor in Bernard. Miss Bianca grew afraid to mention his name, so fiercely the Emperor scowled at its very sound! Obviously to the Emperor Bernard was not only dead as a doornail, but even alive wouldn't have rated much higher than an Adélie. 'We both of us need our understrappers,' observed the Emperor haughtily, 'and of course recognize their usefulness; but if they *will* get themselves frozen to death, surely it needn't interrupt an agreeable conversation!'

Actually no conversation, to Miss Bianca halted once more opposite Theodore the Second, could have been *less* agreeable! As for regarding Bernard as an understrapper, her whiskers prickled to the roots at the thought. Yet how, if she didn't humour the Emperor's obsession, was she ever to persuade him to let her up and out as a first step towards looking for Bernard herself?

At last she had an idea.

2

She began by absolutely *asking* to make the detested tour again; then, just as her gratified host bent to scoop her on his flipper, drew back.

'Oh, dear,' sighed Miss Bianca, 'if only I could give myself up entirely to this delightful experience without another thought in mind!'

'And why can't you?' asked the Emperor, frowning.

But if he expected her to refer to Bernard again, she knew better!

'The privilege of sharing your company,' explained Miss Bianca, 'the example continually before me of your beautiful, thoughtful manners, make me all the more conscious of any deficiency in my *own* . . .' (Of course the Emperor's manners were really quite abominable, but as Benjamin Disraeli once said, everyone likes flattery, and when you come to royalty lay it on with a trowel.) 'It really quite weighs on my mind,' continued Miss Bianca, 'that I never sent the Adélies a note after their Ball . . .' (One should always send a note of thanks after a party. Telephoning isn't the same: to write shows more trouble taken, also one's hostess, telephoned, may be having a bath, or mixing a cake, or for some other reason unwishful to be disturbed.) 'Even the lack of notepaper cannot excuse me,' lamented Miss Bianca, 'for I might still call!'

To her surprise, for she knew his low opinion of Adélies, the Emperor appeared to reflect.

'Indeed, I shouldn't wonder if they never invited me again,' added Miss Bianca, just to underline her point, since she didn't herself truly imagine any continuing social relation with them. She just wanted an excuse to be allowed up and out – any excuse would have done, this simply happened to be the best she could think of, and actually she didn't put much hope in it. But to her surprise again, the Emperor nodded.

'Then you must certainly call,' said he, 'for I mean you to attend *all* the Adélie balls!'

Miss Bianca was not only surprised, she was astounded!

'And by putting in a word here and there,' went on the Emperor, 'you so obviously *persona grata* with them, persuade them they'd be far happier to abandon their self-indulgent, harum-scarum ways and do some useful work.'

'But suppose they don't want to?' objected Miss Bianca sensibly, since so far as she could judge the Adélies' self-indulgence and harum-scarumness were making them perfectly happy already. Certainly it wasn't a way of life she could entirely approve, and one which for herself would have been unthinkable: yet to be happy and at the same time harmless struck her as no bad thing. 'Besides,' she added, 'what useful work is there for them?'

'Why, helping build my statue, of course!' snapped the Emperor. 'Scarcely a generation would suffice, to heap up and build and carve ere I stand for all ages in proper majestic effigy dominating the whole Antarctic mass!'

3

There flashed into Miss Bianca's mind a picture in the Boy's schoolroom, of hundreds and hundreds of slaves whipped on to build a Pharaoh's pyramid. Very different from those sun-dried, emaciated bodies were the plump little figures of the Adélies; but she suddenly glimpsed for them too a similar driven-to-death fate, once indentured to the Emperor Penguin!

'Only suppose they don't want to?' repeated Miss Bianca boldly.

'All I can say is, they'd better!' snapped the Emperor, shutting his beak like a trap. 'As possibly I should have mentioned before, I have only to stamp my foot to blow the whole Antarctic up sky-high! As if I continue to be so frustrated, so I shall! *Then* where would your idle, vulgar friends find themselves – and you too?'

It was now that Miss Bianca for once lost her head. What she ought to have done was pretend to fall in with the Emperor's plans, and then (besides looking for Bernard) *warn* the Adélies of such dreadful, cruel designs upon them. But the picture of those poor driven-to-death Egyptian slaves was still too vivid before her mental eye for her to preserve her customary cool.

'I can still imagine far worser fates!' declared she.

'Such as what?' demanded the Emperor, furiously rearing up to his full height and towering over her with truly awful threateningness.

'Such as being enslaved by a cruel tyrant!' cried Miss Bianca. 'Better far to be blown sky-high whilst still at liberty, as I'm sure the most feckless Adélie would agree! As I too,' cried Miss Bianca, 'would sacrifice all hope of ever seeing my dear Boy again, or Bernard, or any member of the MPAS, sooner than become your *stool-pigeon*! So stamp!'

The Emperor lifted one huge, broad, black-leathery foot, meanwhile bending on her the full force of his burning maniac gaze. For an instant he paused, as though giving her time to quail and change her mind. But little did he know Miss Bianca's mettle! Far from quailing, she stood more gracefully erect than ever; but for the difference in heights they'd have challenged eye-ball to eye-ball, and her own brilliant topaz gaze the bolder!

'I give you a last chance!' cried the Emperor Penguin.

'Phooey!' cried Miss Bianca.

Absolutely infuriated by such insubordination, the Emperor Penguin stamped . . .

'An earthquake in the Antarctic at *this* time of year?' said one seismologist to another. (Seismologists are scientists who specialize in earthquakes as others specialize in tidal waves, or erupting volcanoes, or any other natural disasters.)

'I must say it looks like one,' said his colleague, watching the needle jump up and down on his graph, 'but only minor, wouldn't you think?'

Minor or not, as the whole underground palace cracked and exploded, Miss Bianca was indeed blown sky-high, and so was Bernard. As has been said, only an earthquake could have roused him, and now it did. Up and up flew Bernard and Miss Bianca amid a whole covey of Adélies flying for the first time in their lives, and by a miracle, or the luck of the mice, almost immediately encountered.

'Is that you, Miss Bianca?' gasped Bernard, catching sight of her silvery coat as it showed up bright against a whirling Adélie's black plumage. 'What happiness to see you again, even if as usual in deadly peril! I do hope you've been all right?'

'Perfectly!' Miss Bianca reassured him.

'I'm glad to hear it!' panted Bernard, bouncing off an upside-down Adélie to get closer. 'I couldn't bear to think of it, if you'd been in any way distressed!'

Miss Bianca paused – that is, so far as anyone can pause in the middle of an earthquake. There seemed no point in admitting how truly distressed, how near

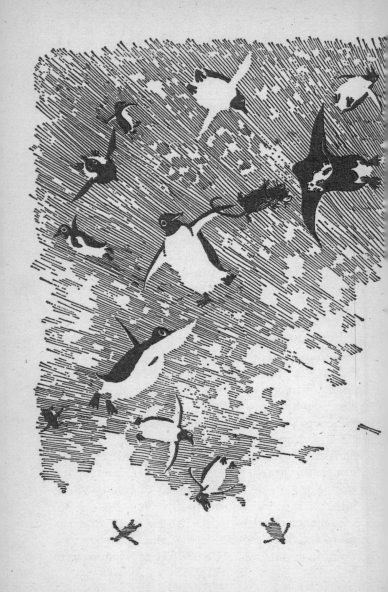

starving, she'd been, in the Emperor Penguin's fell clutch; 'twould only upset Bernard and spoil what she suspected to be their last moments together . . .

'Not in the least!' declared Miss Bianca.

'I'm glad to hear it!' repeated Bernard. 'Especially as this does look rather like the end,' he added, for once as realistic as she, 'of all our adventurings!'

At which instant, confirming their joint apprehensions, to the violent up-draught succeeded as violent a down-draught, sucking both down and down into the pitiless, icy, Antarctic sea . . .

CHAPTER 13

The End

Fortunately, however, it wasn't absolutely into the sea Bernard and Miss Bianca fell, but upon the rim of a red-and-white wreath frozen almost to red-and-white coral, and floating just like a life-belt!

As the Navigator had said, one never knew, with tides . . .

Bernard instantly made good his footing on the next petal – it took his weight. Reaching out to steady Miss Bianca, he found both their weights borne quite easily, by the stalwart chrysanthemums! After hauling her farther aboard, so to speak, he discovered even a tarpaulin – actually a scrap of ribbon upon which only the v of VALE remained unobliterated – sufficient to shelter both of them against the blast for the few moments more ere a helicopter clattered overhead . . .

2

'I don't care for this at all,' said the helicopter captain. 'Turbulence is one thing; *this* feels to me more like an earthquake! So back for home, Navigator!'

The Navigator had no objection. No more had the Hydrographer or the Photographer or the Fisheries-expert. They'd been so bounced about, the

Captain's unheroic words brought rather an expression of cheer to their countenances.

'In fact I couldn't agree more!' said the Navigator, preparing to change course homewards.

But there was still the same Mechanic on board as on the trip when they'd rescued the Poet, and he was still yearning for distinction on account of (another) girl back home.

'Half a mo',' said the Mechanic, peering out, 'what's that down there just below us? It looks to *me* like a life-buoy!'

'So it does,' agreed the Captain, peering out in turn. 'I'm still making for home!'

'No, it doesn't,' said the Mechanic. 'It looks like that great red-and-white job we ditched hundreds and hundreds of miles off! If it is, shouldn't it tell us a bit about currents? Earthquake subsiding, sir, if I could just be winched down and make a grab — ?'

'You're certainly a glutton for punishment,' said the Captain. 'And you may be right at that,' he added thoughtfully. 'At least we'd have something to show for our pains! So down you go, my gallant and intelligent lad, though I warn you we can't allow more than two shakes!'

No longer was needed, for the Mechanic to waver down like a cockchafer on a thread, and then with a strong right arm to grasp the chrysanthemum wreath and bear it (all unwittingly bearing Bernard and Miss Bianca too) safe back!

3

From the helicopter-port the mice had to pick up a bus, but neither minded. Bernard was in any case used to riding buses, and had not Miss Bianca, in the interests of prisoner-rescuing, once actually taken the municipal garbage-van? *In the interests of prisoner-rescuing!* thought Miss Bianca wryly. 'Now 'tis I myself who have needed rescue!' The reflection so acted upon her sensibilities, she felt quite a glow of affection for the honest bus, and pleased Bernard very much by remarking that it was just as warm, if not warmer, than in a private car. (Since they were sitting under the driver's seat just behind the engine, this of course was perfectly true.)

'I've always thought it a good service,' said Bernard, 'especially as us mice seem to be let on free. At least *I*'ve never been asked to show a ticket; per-

haps the Society should send Public Transport some sort of a testimonial?'

How strange it seemed to Miss Bianca, after their desperate adventures in the wholly-public-transportless Antarctic wastes, to find herself suddenly plunged back into all the old ways! Evidently Bernard had taken the plunge more quickly – without noticing, so to speak. But she rather admired him for it, and suggested that the testimonial might even be illuminated.

'As to that, I'll have to have a word with the Treasurer,' said Bernard.

They were home again indeed!

The heat of the engine dried their fur right down to the roots, thawing out the last of the Antarctic chill. Behind them in the body of the bus airport employees chatted, loved ones come to meet loved ones told how much they'd missed them, at stops by the way housewives with shopping-baskets, schoolchildren with satchels, clambered on, and added to the criss-cross of cheerful, everyday conversation. But 'twas only when Bernard in his most worried ex-Secretary voice spoke of consulting the Treasurer that Miss Bianca felt herself truly home!

Tripping down beside him at the stop opposite the Embassy, she lightly brushed his whiskers with her own, which so acted upon *his* sensibilities, he got off on the wrong foot and took a purler, but fortunately there wasn't much traffic about.

What a joyful reunion was Miss Bianca's with the Boy, whom she found watering the Pagoda pleasure-garden with a slight sniffle! Of course he was too big to cry, but without an almost daily sniffle all her precious seedlings would have quite withered, so she felt fonder of him than ever.

'Oh, Miss Bianca,' cried the Boy, 'wherever have you been?'

'Just in the Antarctic,' said Miss Bianca.

'Where the polar bears are?' asked the Boy eagerly.

'However many times must I remind you,' said Miss Bianca, 'that polar bears live at the *North* Pole, not the South?'

(There was obviously no point in confusing his mind with Exchange Visits, especially after seeing how bad his Geography marks were while she was away.)

'I hope you enjoyed yourself all the same,' said the Boy, rather reproachfully. 'I must say you look prettier and fluffier than ever, Miss Bianca!' Then he squeezed her. 'Only how *thin* you've grown!' he added. 'Are you certain you're quite all right?'

'Perfectly,' Miss Bianca reassured him, just as she'd reassured Bernard. 'Now put me down and let me look round my garden, which I'm so pleased to see hasn't been neglected!'

The Boy opened the Pagoda gate for her, and in

she ran. Everything was in order, all her seedlings were doing quite beautifully, and there beside the fountain what should meet her astonished gaze but a quite new feature in the shape of a bent-match-wood rocking-chair!

'Why, how did *that* get here?' asked Miss Bianca.

'Thomas Footman found it in the wine-cellar,' explained the Boy, 'by one of the old wine-casks, and when he brought it up as a curiosity I thought it was just your size. You won't ever go away again, will you, Miss Bianca?' begged the Boy. 'I've been so worried I had to be X-rayed!'

'Never!' promised Miss Bianca, subsiding grace-fully, also exhaustedly, into the once-odious gift of the MPAS Arts and Handicrafts Centre . . .

5

Bernard found his cigar-cabinet flat in as good order as Miss Bianca's garden, and soon straightened things out with the Dairy.

The helicopter captain, instead of being blamed for not completing his last mission, received a Good Service medal for bringing back (via the chrysanthemum wreath) what turned out to be quite important information about tides and currents.

The Mechanic, upon the Captain's recommendation, was promoted to Chief Mechanic, and so was able to marry his girl at home without further delay. If it wasn't the same girl he'd originally wished to impress when he was winched down and rescued the Poet, she was even prettier and nicer, and in due course bore him four sons, all of whom, in further due course, became Chief Mechanics too.

The Poet, safe back in Oslo, never joined a scientific expedition again. Once was quite enough for him. But he composed a Saga about his harrowing experiences which was so much more exciting than anything else he'd ever written, it became highly popular both in print and as a recitation, and after living for years on bread and cheese (like most poets), he could now have sausages every other Sunday.

Nils, that vagabond of the seas, actually hadn't taken passage home at all, owing to the attractions of a South-bound schooner. Even though it was off Java he'd lost his leg, the Tropic Isles still called, and when his sailing days were at last done he settled beneath the palm-trees as a mouse-beachcomber.

Humbert after returning with his parents to their proper habitat in the Arctic forgot Miss Bianca rather soon; he was rapidly growing too big to believe in Fairies. But his mother, as has been said, always remembered the tale of 'The Three Loving Brothers', and spread it through every northern bear- or kinder-garten.

As for the little Adélies, though after the earthquake some were never seen again, they were so numerous, also feckless, an odd aunt or uncle or cousin or two was scarcely missed, and a new figure invented by the caller known as Earthquakes —

'Up and up now high we fly
Bounce your partner till she hits the sky!'

— became almost as popular as Pebbles.

They were never indentured into the Emperor's cruel service. Only someone the Adélies admired as much as they did Miss Bianca had the least chance of persuading them into it, and she, as has been seen, wouldn't even try. In any case the Emperor was now blown quite finally sky-high, which served him right.

Meditating a new poem in her newly-discovered verse-form Miss Bianca rocked at ease, at last enjoying all the total-repose-and-security Bernard had envisaged for her. But what made her happiest of all was the knowledge that against however terrible odds, he and she had rescued *themselves*!

Mr Popper's Penguins

FLORENCE AND RICHARD ATWATER

All through the summer Mr Popper paints people's houses, but when winter comes, he stays at home reading books on polar exploration. Mr Popper longs to be an explorer, and this leads him to write a letter to his hero Admiral Drake at the South Pole. In return Admiral Drake sends him a present – marked 'Keep Cool' – which contains a lively penguin named Captain Cook who moves into the fridge. But this is only the beginning . . . before long, there are eleven more penguins in the Popper household!

'These events are treated as normal and quite understandable happenings, and the humour arises from this matter of fact acceptance, which appeals greatly to children.'

Sheila Ray, Children's Fiction

'It bounces gaily from hilarity to hilarity.' *School Librarian*

Delightful reading for sevens and up.

The Hunting
of Wilberforce Pike

MOLLY LEFEBURE

Wilberforce Pike is a cruel, red-whiskered, cat-thief, who snatches unsuspecting felines to be made into fur coats. Oliver Simpkin, a previously sheltered pet, is one of Pike's first captives, but the fearless Power Station gang comes to his rescue and saves his skin. He joins them in the mysterious cat underworld and swears to bring revenge on the villain Pike and his equally sinister wife. And so the mad chase begins . . .

This is an extremely funny book, with a strong, adventurous story-line, for readers of ten upwards.

'A refreshing and hilarious story with some unforgettable characters.'   *Eastern Daily Mail*

Baba and Mr Big

C. EVERARD PALMER

Milo's face lit up. 'Well, you have to pass the test. You have
to catch that hawk. Do it and you join up. Don't and you stay
out.'

Jim Anderson was incredulous. To become one of the gang
he had to catch that mighty smart, swooping, chicken-killing
hawk – alive!

But it had to be done. New as he was to the village of
Kendal, Jamaica, how else could he join in with the other
boys, be part of their games, their fun. So he accepts the
challenge with the help and encouragement of old Baba, and
together they outwit the bully boys.

'An exuberantly funny yarn.'   *Children's Book of the Year*

'This is a voice that seemed to have gone out with E. Nesbit,
Mark Twain and Stevenson. Mr Palmer is surely a find.'
                                        Times Literary Supplement

Along Came a Dog

MEINDERT DEJONG

The little red hen was different from all the other hens in the barnyard, and that made her an outcast. She was cocky and mean, but she needed protection. At least that's what the big black dog thought. So he became her slave. He was at the little hen's beck and call. With a swipe of his paw he sent her enemy, the weasel, packing! And a growl drove the squawking rooster away in terror!

He stole eggs from the other hens for her to sit on. Then one day she had five little chicks. The big black dog had a family at last!

Shadrach and *Journey from Peppermint Street* are both Lions. For eight-year-olds and upwards.